LEFTY AND THE KILLERS

Trevor Holliday

Barnstork Press

ISBN-13: 9798764028873
ISBN-10: 1477123456

Cover design by: John M. Holliday
Library of Congress Control Number: 2018675309
Printed in the United States of America

To Marvin Minkler

CONTENTS

THE MARINA CAROUSEL LOUNGE

Florida began to get on Lefty's nerves from the start of late spring until early summer when he would head home to Cutler, Maine.

Back during his baseball career Lefty would have been assigned to a minor league team by now. In all of his years in pro ball, Lefty had never made an opening day roster. He made a career out of being a mid-season call-up, coming up from the bushes to eat up innings in games already lost.

Now, with his playing days over, Lefty stayed in Florida a little longer each year, liking it less and less as the temperature increased.

By early May this year Lefty had already quit his job as greeter and security at the Marina Carousel Lounge in Daytona.

He spent a couple of days walking the beach, weighing the pros and cons of buying a metal detector.

There would be no down time, that was a pro.

He could use the device all year long, whether he was in Maine or in Florida.

You never knew what you would find when walking on the beach. Coins, even valuable antique ones. Lefty pictured himself on a page in *Life*, tanned and happy, holding up a handful of valuable doubloons, or better yet, a whole chest filled with them.

Lefty Strikes Gold, the article would read.

Ex-Pitcher Finds Fortune on Beaches.

On the other hand, Lefty was already tanned, and he was happy most of the time anyway.

By buying a metal detector, Lefty would be committing to picking up beer tabs, spent bottle rockets, and other useless metal debris. He imagined the feeling of defeat after each fruitless day of beach combing.

Nobody using a metal detector looked particularly cheerful. Purchasing one could be a ticket to drudgery.

After a few days on the beach, Lefty packed his Winnebago.

Ginger Manley, the proprietress of the Marina Carousel Lounge took Lefty's resignation in stride.

"It's fine, Lefty," she said, "Fine. It's not like you were the last of the red hot lovers, anyway."

Lefty cringed. He had always kept his relationship with Ginger professional.

It was the time of evening when Ginger tended to start slurring words about Sarasota over gin and tonics.

"You're right, business is slow," Ginger said. "I mighta hadda cut down your hours anyway before too long. You know you can always come back next year, honey. It's nice to have somebody I can count on. It's different now than the way it was when I was in the circus."

She stopped herself. Swirled the ice in her drink with the tip of her index finger.

"*With* the circus, I mean, not in it. There's a difference. Back then, I knew you were coming back if you were in the show, you know what I mean?"

It wasn't Ginger's first obscure circus reference. She kept *Circus Report* newsletters in her office next to her Kent cigarettes. Sometimes Lefty saw Ginger had circled items in the classified advertisements.

Lefty found out about Ginger's circus background in a circuitous way. On a slow day during the first winter he worked at the lounge, Lefty had pulled out his Marine Band harmonica and played a few bars of a Stephen Foster song. There were no customers at all in the lounge, and frankly, Lefty had done it unconsciously.

Ginger screamed at him.

"Put that damn thing away," she said, pointing at the harmonica. Lefty quickly dropped it back in his pocket.

"Don't you have any sense at all?" she said. "Those things bring terrible, terrible luck."

Later in the day, Frankie, who had seen the whole incident explained Ginger's explosion.

"It's the circus, Lefty," Frankie said. "That's one of the most serious no-nos you can make under the big top. Circus folk think harmonicas bring disaster. Tell you the truth I feel funny even talking about it."

Frankie went back to the game of solitaire he'd been playing and offered no further explanation.

Lefty didn't exactly know what Ginger meant by the comments she made about him leaving, but he winked at her on the way out, anyway.

He quit the lounge every year at the same time. Back to Maine before Memorial Day, return to Florida after the hurricanes. Not quite like his life in baseball, but close enough.

He wasn't leaving Ginger stranded. By the end of the early spring, there wasn't anybody to greet. No audience for his baseball stories. By then they had all gone home. The only security needed was to nudge the regulars from their barstool perches and head them toward home at closing time.

Anyway, Ginger had her boyfriend Frankie who had done advance tickets for a well known animal circus. Frankie was a stocky guy with heavy glasses who performed close up magic and card tricks. Lefty had learned the hard way not to get into a card game with Frankie. Frankie could rig even the simplest game of chance, and would. If anybody needed greeting over the summer, Frankie would take care of things.

TAVERNA ATHENA

The Taverna Athena Diner opened every day except Sunday at six in the morning, but every morning Tad Karras came in long before that on account of the coffee and to make sure everything in his diner was just right.

Tad knew he could be a little fussy, but he didn't feel right unless he personally made sure everything was spic and span from the night before.

You never knew when the health inspectors would come down to South Portland from Augusta to take a look around the place. Tad ran a clean diner and he wanted the place to keep its top health inspection rating.

On the curb, the AMC Gremlin Tad had bought was parked, ready to make deliveries today all over the city.

The car sparkled from a recent trip through the car wash. Max and Al, the two dopes Tad had hired for deliveries, ran the Gremlin through nearly every other day. In the summer months the car showed off nicely with the trademarked *LUSTRE-COTE* treatment. More important were the winter *MAXI-COTE SPARKLE* treatments to combat the salt on the South Portland streets.

When it came to car maintenance, Tad's philosophy was that you could never spend enough on prevention.

Tad liked the lines of the Gremlin. The car was modern and space-aged and projected the kind of image Tad wanted for his place. And if he was going to put the Taverna Athena signs on the side, the car needed to shine.

❉ ❉ ❉

It was a shame Bobby didn't see things the same way.

Tad was proud of his brother, but frustrated by him at the same time. The kid lived in the past. Still talking about the island. Maybe even talking about going back some day for good.

What kind of idea was that? There was nothing for either of them on that island. Tad was glad his parents had brought them here and was just sad they didn't live to see what he'd made of this business.

What kind of idea was going back to Symi? It was a crazy idea. Tad told Bobby what a crazy idea it was every time Bobby said something about it.

Both of the brothers had everything they

needed here. This was the land of opportunity.

Bobby would grow out of it. Tad figured it was just a phase his brother was going through.

✳ ✳ ✳

Tad put on the coffee in the Bunn machine then sat in the booth next to the jukebox.

He had Larry, the guy who serviced the jukebox add the *Zorba* theme.

Mikis Theodorakas. In Tad's book, the composer of *Zorba* was a genius.

Tad played it sometimes late at night when he felt sentimental and he was drinking a couple of shots. Sometimes, like today, he played it in the morning to set a mood.

The guys were coming today.

These guys didn't want Tad making a fuss over their visits. Besides Tad's little brother Bobby, nobody knew about these guys.

Gus Pappas and his brother Mike would just take a coffee and maybe spend a couple of minutes chatting, if that.

That was okay with Tad. The less song and dance the better.

Truthfully, he didn't even spend too much time thinking about the arrangement. Gus and Mike brought the money and Tad did what he needed to do. It was easy for Tad to account for the money they brought. The Taverna Athena did a good business both in the diner and in deliveries. Everybody won the way they had things lined up. Gus and Mike got what they needed and Tad had been able to buy the diner easily.

Tad also got to pocket a large amount of his own revenue, because compared to the money Gus and Mike brought him, it was small potatoes, right?

Tad didn't advertise the arrangement. Nobody needed to know what was his own business.

Sure, Bobby knew some of what was going on, but that was okay. Bobby was Tad's little brother, and if you couldn't trust him, who could you trust?

Everything was hunky dory. The Taverna Athena was just a small place. Not too many moving parts. Tad had a good morning crew with Bobby and Iris plus Al and Max, the two delivery dopes.

He wondered if he was going to have to do something about those two.

Especially Max. You can't have somebody around you don't trust.

Then again, Tad had always heard the devil you know is better than the one you don't.

Max was just there to do deliveries, and, Tad had to admit, Max was pretty good at it.

Better than his buddy Al, who got Max the job.

Tad figured it was better to just let things stay put.

Tad was used to hard work. Long hours and hard work. That's the way you get ahead. That was another part of Tad's philosophy.

With the diner, Tad was his own man, making his own decisions.

Gus and Mike showed up about a minute or two early. They looked like a couple guys heading out for an early morning eighteen holes maybe at one of the swanky courses. Gus had on a blue and green Golden Bear golf shirt. Mike, the one with heavy eyebrows, wore lime green pants and a salmon red sweater.

"Coffee, fellas?" Tad said. They had come in the back from the kitchen's back door when Tad opened it. Tad always offered them coffee.

"Naah, no coffee for me," Gus said.

Mike stretched, then said sure, why not, but wanted it in a paper cup. Screwing the lid on the cup, Mike nosed up to the glass pie tower.

Pointed at the baklava.

"Is that fresh?" he said.

"Are you kidding," Tad said. "Lemme get you a couple."

Tad cut a couple of pieces off, put them in a foam container, handed it to Mike who held it up to his nose and sniffed. Mike smiled.

✣ ✣ ✣

Tad didn't like seeing Max coming through the door.

This was exactly the wrong time. This bozo had to pick today to come in early?

Max Hellman. Dope Number One.

Max was walking into the diner wearing some kind of disco getup.

First thing in the morning.

Not a good outfit for making deliveries. Tad knew he'd have to say something about the clothes.

Max Hellman. Hellman, like the mayo, which was the first thing Tad thought when he had looked at Max's application.

He never should have hired Max.

Max's tight beige suit looked like he'd slept in it.

He was planning to wear this for deliveries?

Gus looked at Max. Turned toward Tad.

"What's this, Tad? You got Saturday Night Fever here this morning?"

Max grinned. His eyes really were crazy.

He looked at Gus and Mike.

"You and Arnold Palmer playing golf today?"

Gus was a golf fanatic. Once the snow melted, Gus kept his clubs in the back of his car every day.

"Hey Max," Tad said, "get the hell out of here, okay? Go out back and count pizza boxes or something."

Max shrugged and went into the kitchen.

Tad turned to Gus and Max.

"I'm sorry fellas. This clown isn't supposed to be here this early."

Gus waved his hand. It was nothing to Gus and Mike.

Tad slumped back. Relieved.

Gus brought out the big envelope.

Always the envelope.

"There's a little more than usual today. Take a look. See if you can handle it."

Tad made the count. It was a lot more than usual.

This was the part Tad didn't particularly care for. Tad was fastidious, and the money was grubby.

Being in the food business, Tad was a hand washer.

Tad finished the count and then grinned.

"You're not kidding," Tad said. "That's a lotta souvlaki."

Gus knit his eyebrows.

"Is this a problem, Thaddeus?"

Tad laughed.

"Not a problem. Just means things are good, right?"

They slapped him on the back. Both of them. Gus and Mike.

Tad wasn't worried about the cash.

The cash presented absolutely no problem to Tad at all.

He'd been worried about Max, but Max didn't seem to bother the Pappas brothers.

* * *

When they left, Tad did what he always did. He took stacks of money, shook them into a couple of zip-locked plastic freezer bags before putting them in the brown leather overnight bag.

He placed the bag next to him in the booth.

He grabbed a cup of coffee and sat for a while not thinking about anything in particular.

Pushed D-14. Tad never let Larry take that song off the jukebox.

Years ago, a Conway Twitty record made it to Symi. The taverna on the beach played it over and over and Tad associated the song with America.

He looked at the photograph of Symi on the wall next to the booth.

Twitty's strong voice climbed from one key to another.

It's Only Make Believe.

The picture showed Saint Nicholas Beach. Tad looked at the blaze of white sand and the bright blue sea. Beautiful. With the song on the jukebox, Tad felt like he was back there as a kid.

He'd told Bobby about his early days on the island. Sometimes the two of them swam together in the freezing water of Penobscot Bay. There were islands ringing the bay and it was salt water, but it wasn't much like Symi.

It was funny. Bobby didn't remember much about the old country, but he was the one who wanted to go back.

Tad looked at the photograph again. He knew he would go back there someday.

Just not yet.

He would only go back as a rich man.

* * *

Max came out of the kitchen and grinned at Tad.

Stood next to the booth looking down at Tad.

Max's eyes were crazy. Tad knew he should have payed closer attention to something like Max's eyes. It didn't make any difference if the guy was quick with the deliveries, Tad was going to fire him.

Him and his stoner buddy, Al.

"Big day for you, Tad?"

He couldn't have Max around here. It wasn't good for business at all. You take a guy with eyes like that, you're gonna lose business.

"What the hell are you doing here, Max?" Tad said. "You're not working. The place is closed.."

Max snapped his fingers and laughed.

"You should be dancing," he said.

Tad shook his head. He would definitely fire Max. Too bad about Al. Tough.

"Get it?" Max said. "You should be dancing."

Max kept the grin on his face, fluttering eyeball and all.

He held up a gun and pointed at the bag.

"What's in the bag, Tad? Those guys brought something. Mind I take a look?"

WAITING FOR BOBBY KARRAS

Iris Cassidy came in early. She didn't see Tad Karras's dead body at first.

She'd been in the Taverna Athena for a couple of minutes and was too far into the diner to be able to retreat when she saw Tad's blood-soaked body slumped in a booth near the jukebox.

Max Hellman was standing next to the jukebox with the gun.

Max's eye was fluttering.

❋ ❋ ❋

The diner was shaped like an L.

All you saw when you first stepped in the front door was a line of padded stools under the long lunch counter.

None of the regulars ate in the front room. The regulars sat in the back room in booths lining the walls and at tables set with brown glass ashtrays, vases filled with fake flowers, and at night, chianti bottles with the dripping candles.

There was a pool table in the back room, a juke box, and the swinging doors leading to the kitchen.

That's where everybody sat at the Taverna Athena, and that was where Tad's body lay prone in the third booth on the kitchen side of the room.

So that was why Iris couldn't see Tad Karras when she first walked in, and why she hadn't turned around and run out the door.

She would have run if she had seen him.

But she didn't run because she hadn't see him or Max.

❉ ❉ ❉

Max, drinking a twenty-four ounce can of Schlitz Malt Liquor, stood across from Tad's body, just acting as if this kind of thing happened every day.

He wasn't even holding the gun, but it was close to him.

Max looked at Iris. She noticed the fluttering thing was only in one of his eyes.

"Hey Iris," he said.

He held up the can of malt liquor.

"You want one of these?"

❉ ❉ ❉

She didn't scream. That's what she remembered later. She remembered not screaming when she saw Tad.

Iris took in every detail. Butcher paper menus, Budweiser signs, Little League team photos lining the walls. A framed newspaper article which described Tad as an asset to the South Portland, Maine community.

For some reason, Iris focused on the butcher paper. The menus were part of Iris's daily tasks, writing up new lunch specials like liver and onions and chili mac.

She didn't have to change the sandwich standbys like fried egg, egg salad, tuna salad, any more than she had to drop the gyros and souvlaki.

Biggest thing she had to change were the puddings, pies, and jello dishes, all of them written out in her careful script Tad liked.

Black marker on white paper so you could read it from across the room.

Tad had complimented her on her handwriting more than once.

"You got nice handwriting, Iris," Tad had said. "You oughtta try writing some Greek."

Iris focused on the menus, she guessed, so she wouldn't have to look at Tad.

❉ ❉ ❉

Tad was as Greek as you could get.

He looked like that guy Michael Constantine from *Room 222*. Iris used to watch that show on the little black and white TV in the living room in Houlton. Tad had heavy eyebrows and the shoulders of a wrestler.

His brother Bobby was a whole different story. Bobby looked like John Travolta used to look before *Saturday Night Fever* came out. Back when Travolta was on *Welcome Back Kotter*.

Bobby was Tad's little brother, but they didn't look anything like each other.

Bobby liked Iris and Iris liked Bobby, but Bobby was too young for Iris.

Bobby was just a kid, but he was fun to play around with and there wasn't any harm in that, was there?

* * *

She had come into the diner early.

If she'd come in later it might have been Bobby who walked in on Max with the gun.

And if she'd come in earlier, maybe Tad would still be alive.

What could she have done either way? If you believed in fate, nothing.

Iris never came in this early, but she did this morning.

She remembered what Tad told her when he hired her.

"You handle the coffee. Bobby and I do the cooking. Stay out of things that don't concern you."

It was the regular speech he gave new girls, Iris figured.

Tad had hired her almost immediately when she came in to fill out an application.

"Lemme see what you got so far," Tad had said, looking at her application. She'd started writing, using a green ballpoint pen and her best handwriting. She had been thinking about the questions on the application and whether or not she really wanted Tad to contact any of her previous employers. Then the green ink had started to poop out.

"Don't bother," Tad had said when he picked up the application from under her pen.

"Nice handwriting," he said.

She hadn't even gotten half way through the application and she wasn't sure if this was a good or bad thing. She had skipped ahead, past the experience and education part. She was wondering about references.

What did she want to say about the last places she had worked? Iris hated these questions. It wasn't as if she had things to hide. She didn't, but she also didn't want to have long conversations about things that made no difference in the job for which she was applying.

Tad was not heavy, but he had the big shoulders and a thick neck. The day she applied for the job,

Bobby had been cooking and Tad had been wearing heavy silver cufflinks etched with a couple of black Greek letters she didn't know.

"Iris is your name?"

Tad had picked up the application and glanced at it before dropping it on the opposite side of the table.

"You're Greek?" he said. "That's a good thing,"

Iris wasn't Greek.

Her family came from Houlton, Maine, and before that, from rural New Brunswick.

French mother, Irish father.

Home life for Iris had been volatile at times, and Iris had left after high school graduation.

* * *

Iris knew something was wrong almost as soon as she came into the diner.

She couldn't identify the smell of gunpowder hanging in the air from the discharged gun. Not then, anyway.

All she had was a feeling of foreboding.

She knew something wasn't right.

* * *

Iris didn't speak French, at least not the way her grandmother did.

Iris had left Houlton driving the Volare her brother said she could use while he was in the army.

"Feel free to use it," he said.

"Watch out for that," he said, pointing at the rust hole on the passenger's side door panel. "You can get fumes. You don't want to puke from that."

He'd lifted the hood of the car and pointed his chin back at the family home on River Street.

"You ever wanna get outta this place, just keep putting oil right in here about every couple hundred miles. Doesn't matter what kinda oil. Whatever's on sale."

Iris took Route 1 out of Houlton on a sunny day a few years before, heading south past Grand Lake. Skirting the Haynesville Woods. She ended up as far as she could get Down East.

Eastport, Maine. The first city in the country to see the sun rise.

She had some money. She thought she would eventually go from Eastport out to the west coast. Iris had never been there, but she'd seen California all her life on television. The place would be a real-life *Wonderful World of Color.*

As a stop-gap measure, she got a job in Eastport, waitressing in a place where summer tourists ordered lobsters and fried clams.

She didn't wait for winter, when she knew the only business would be local guys who drank Narragansetts in the diner's dark bar.

She knew what winters in Houlton were like.

Long cold and dark. Eastport, located on an island with all sides exposed to ocean, would only be worse.

She left when the red leaves had mostly fallen from the trees.

Her brother's Volare made it to South Carolina, then died. Three things on the car went bad all at once. Alternator, brakes, and starter. The rust hole on the passenger's side hadn't affected the operation of the vehicle, but now the car wouldn't run.

The mechanic, wiping his hands on his pants coming out of the garage told her how much the repairs would be and Iris knew it would be cheaper to save her money and buy another car.

"I never seen a Volare that was worth a damn. Not even once," the mechanic said.

He refused Iris's offer of payment.

"Don't need it," he said. "I was in the service myself."

Iris found another job in another diner and sent a letter to her brother about the car, promising she would pay for it eventually. She wasn't surprised when she got a letter back from him. He was now a tracked vehicle mechanic at Fort Sill, Oklahoma and in his letter he said life was working out well for him and Iris didn't need to worry about the car. It had been on its last legs anyway, and he was surprised the car had lasted that long.

He said he was glad he had her address. He might send her some money, but it would be awhile before he could.

Even though the army was tough duty sometimes, he said, he was glad to be away from Houlton in the winter.

＊ ＊ ＊

Tad's body lay across the vinyl seat of his booth face down.

He looked like a man reaching for coins he had dropped on the floor.

The bullet holes were punched in his body and there were bloodstains on the seat.

The horror of the scene brought Iris's hands to her mouth.

＊ ＊ ＊

"Whattya think, baby?"

Max Hellman had taken a seat in the opposite booth. Dangling the gun between his legs now, the can of malt liquor on the table. A brown leather bag next to him.

"Something you don't see every day, is it?" Max said.

She took a step toward Tad's body then leaned against the closest chair. Her mouth opened in a silent scream.

"It's a shame you got here so early," Max said. He lifted the gun up. "Then again, maybe a shame you weren't here a few minutes earlier."

He waved his gun at Tad's body. "You shoulda seen him."

Iris had buried her face in her hands. She could barely see Max.

His words were slurred. She saw another twenty-four ounce can lying crumpled and empty on the floor.

Max got up and took a step closer to her. Taking a step away from Tad's body. Holding the gun loosely he pulled a cigarette from his coat pocket. Lighted it then walked up to the jukebox.

"Stay right there, baby," he said. "You want a drink or something?"

He pulled some coins from his pocket. Dropped a couple in the jukebox.

"Hey," he said. "Whattya like on this thing? I like to see you dance."

Iris felt a pain start to well in her stomach. The room felt claustrophobic.

She tried collecting her thoughts. She had only one chance to escape. She might not even have that.

Nobody on the street could see this part of the diner. They were in the bottom of an L shaped room. Booths, a jukebox, pool table in the other room.

From the plate glass windows in front, everything would look normal.

She wasn't far from the swinging doors leading to the kitchen. Iris thought about the kitchen. Bobby's domain. The grill, the walk-in fridge, the big aluminum dishwasher with the hanging nozzle.

Knives.

The back door.

The back door where Bobby could walk in any time.

"Come on baby," Max said. "I wanna see you dance."

He held the gun toward her while looking at the selections on the jukebox.

The back door.

If Bobby came in now, Max would kill him.

Max wouldn't hesitate before killing Bobby, just the same way he'd killed Tad.

Just the same way Max could kill her.

The automatic mechanism in the jukebox selected the record, cradled it, then dropped it on to a forty-five rpm turntable.

The Bee Gees singing falsetto.

You Should Be Dancing.

❈ ❈ ❈

If Max would kill Tad, he would kill Bobby. Iris knew that just like she knew Bobby would come through the front door of the Taverna Athena like he always did in the morning.

Fresh for the new day with his crazy attitude

and stupid jokes.

Unless he'd partied the night before and then Iris would have to avoid Bobby the first couple hours until he felt good enough to start working.

Iris didn't mind doing that. Bobby looked so pathetic holding his head in one of the booths. She'd bring him a bottle of Coke from the cooler and some aspirin from her purse. It didn't happen all too often, and Bobby was appreciative as hell, pleading with Iris not to tell Tad.

Bobby was a good kid and Iris liked him. She didn't like him as much as Bobby would have liked, and not the way he would have liked. Bobby was like a younger brother to Iris.

❋ ❋ ❋

Max opened another can of malt liquor. He kept the can in one hand and the gun in the other.

Tight tan bell-bottoms Max wore and a flowered polyester shirt open to the fourth button to show off sparse chest hair.

He was doing something with the jukebox, but he had his eye on Iris too.

"I'm sick of this song, aren't you?" Max said. "You probably like disco though, am I right? You like disco, don't you?"

Iris watched him.

She couldn't let Bobby get killed.

Max was a psychopath.

Tad's dead body slumped in the booth didn't bother Max at all.

Max's attention was focused on the jukebox. Looking over the selections.

She could maybe get to the kitchen. Get a knife. Then what?

"Got plenty of disco, if that's what you like. Got some Ohio Players here," he said. "You like that? Hot Chocolate?"

She took a quick look at the doors to the kitchen.

"You could make some money, Iris," Max said. "Stripping. Even skinny you can make some bread, you know?"

He wasn't watching her. She might make the kitchen.

"Come on baby," he said. "Go ahead. Nobody here but the two of us. Just you and me, Iris. Just you and me. And buh-baby makes three."

Iris slipped out of her shoes. Moved a little to the music.

Max was watching her now.

"That's it," Max said. "Put some damn feeling in it."

Max put the gun on the table in front of himself. Snapped his fingers.

Was Max daring her to try picking up the gun? She wasn't nearly close enough to try.

"Where's Al?" Iris said.

She swayed a little. Not too much.

She said it again a little louder to be heard over

the music.

"He couldn't make it, Al couldn't," Max said. "He had a previous engagement. That's why it's just you and me. The two of us. Why you wanna know?"

"I thought you two went everywhere together," Iris said. "You and Al. I'm not used to seeing you alone."

"What's that supposed to mean," Max said. "What are you saying?"

Iris shrugged. Forced herself to at least try to look calm.

"You saying something funny about me and Al? Is that what you're trying to say?"

"Nothing, Max," she said. "Just asking. Making conversation."

"It's just the two of us here, okay? Get used to it, baby," Max said. "Get used to it."

He picked up the gun again. Iris's spirits fell.

Max's gun was an automatic.

She wished she had her gun with her.

She had gotten out of the habit of carrying it.

It wasn't doing her any good right now.

She could never have picked up the gun in front of Max. He'd placed it too far from her.

If she had reached for it, Iris knew she would be dead too, lying in the booth next to Tad.

Iris was just waiting for Bobby to come in.

"Put a little more feeling into it," Max said. "A little more *oomph*."

Max grinned. He held his hands up to encourage

her like he was a choreographer.

The song changed to Boz Scaggs. Iris knew this album well.

Silk Degrees.
Lowdown.

KING OF THE GYPSIES

Not too fast, Lefty kept reminding himself. He had left Florida's A-1-A after Fernandina Beach and gotten on I-95

Even though the Winnebago seemed solid, these things had a high center of gravity and Lefty didn't want the recreational vehicle to pitch into the highway barriers like an errant knuckleball.

Through northern Georgia and through much of South Carolina, Lefty kept telling himself he had just spent his last winter at the Marina Carousel Lounge.

Camping in a primitive site in the middle of the Francis Marion National Forest, Lefty felt like the Swamp Fox himself, watching fireflies and eating a warmed-up can of Dinty Moore canned beef stew.

Lefty played his harmonica after dinner. It felt good to play the Marine Band with impunity. He was considering his options for the months too cold to spend on the coast of Maine.

Next year, he'd make more of an effort to find a better place to work in Florida. He could easily find another security job. Nobody really wanted to work for Ginger. Even Ginger with her circus newsletter was looking for something else.

Somehow Lefty had drifted into security. He intuitively sensed trouble before it happened.

He had gotten to know Ginger shortly after she had been victimized by a very skinny man from the Augusta area who had offered to hot-top the parking area of her lounge.

He had stopped in the lounge to make a phone call and she'd given him the story over an umbrella drink.

"Honestly, Lefty," she had said, "I got taken by one of the oldest gypsy con-games in the book. I shoulda known better seeing him and those jailbird tattoos he had. Homemade rolling dice on the left arm? I mean come on. I shoulda known better. But you know? I got taken in. Funny thing is, I spent so much time with the circus, I forgot once I retired, I was just another rube."

All the tar the man poured on Ginger's driveway had run off onto her little patch of lawn.

It didn't take long for Lefty to track down the skinny man.

He lived in a motel room outside of Mims.

Lefty watched the place from a nearby Tasty-Freeze. The man lived in the room by himself. That surprised Lefty, who had figured any man working an asphalt scam would lived communally. He had expected a lady telling fortunes at least, but there was nothing like that in the small wood paneled motel room.

The man didn't put up much of a fight.

He answered the door when Lefty knocked on it, smoking a Kool and holding a Mickey's Big Mouth.

Over the man's shoulder Lefty saw a gold ceramic cobra coiled next to the television.

The Newlywed Game was playing. Bob Eubanks was laughing at a woman with a beehive hairdo who was bashing her husband over the head with a piece of cardboard.

The skinny man postured a little. He had picked up the ceramic cobra and threatened Lefty with the serpent's evil eye.

He didn't hold up well to the pressure Lefty put on his right arm.

The money was hidden in a Chock full o'Nuts can in the back of the man's van.

Ginger insisted Lefty take a cut for the recovery.

"I mean your time's worth something, isn't it Lefty?" Ginger said.

"Sure," Lefty had said. "Why not. I'll keep the can, too."

That was the start of Lefty's security career.

Truthfully, Lefty didn't even need the small amount of money Ginger Manley would stuff into a Carousel Club envelope for him each Friday. Every week Ginger would pay him like this. She had given him an extra envelope a couple of days before Christmas and Lefty put it all in the Chock full o'Nuts can.

"You save me this much do-re-mi," Ginger said. "You're worth your weight in gold, and then some."

Lefty didn't argue. Ginger was right, but still, he'd been reluctant to take permanent employment back then, and he was still thinking over the pros and cons of continuing at the Carousel.

He would have preferred to be one of those guys who rode off into the sunset. So far though, things hadn't worked out that way.

Lefty had taken Ginger's Christmas bonus and found the closest Salvation Army bell ringer. The guy had been ringing the bell over one of those kettles on a tripod. A skinny guy who looked a lot like the gypsy but without the homemade rolling dice tattoo. Lefty didn't even try to stuff the bills in the small slot at the top of the kettle. Instead, he walked directly up to the guy and handed him the money directly.

"Merry Christmas," Lefty said. "Skip the middle-man. This is for you."

* * *

Pulling out of the National Forest, and driving through Charleston, South Carolina, Lefty realized he was only trying to fool himself. He liked routine.

He got out of the car and walked around the old

streets of Charleston, stopping for crab legs and a beer.

His life had taken on a predictable pattern he wasn't uncomfortable with.

Lefty knew he'd be back at the Carousel Club next winter.

THE STRIPPER

Iris had never stripped before and she didn't want to start now.

Not with Max's fluttering eye focused on her. Not with the gun in his hands.

She was stalling for time, hoping it didn't look obvious.

"Come on baby," Max said. "What are you waiting for?"

She turned her back to him. Closed her eyes.

She put her fingers on the top button of her blouse.

The button unfastened easily.

Boz Scaggs kept singing.

Iris raised her hands over her head then let her fingers run through her curly dark hair.

This was an impossible situation.

Iris had seen a television program where a woman and a man discussed a technique for relaxation. She remembered the man looked like Dick Cavett, but spoke with a Scandinavian accent. The show had been more of a commercial than a program, because the woman kept interrupting to make an offer for tapes which could be purchased through the mail, but Iris had tried as much of the technique as she could glean without calling the number on the screen. She was visualizing a place of comfort. Feeling each cell in her body relaxing.

Iris kept her eyes closed. She tried.

She really did try. She breathed in and breathed out.

Focusing on the task in front of her, slowly unbuttoning her front, all the time knowing the relaxation technique was not going to work.

IT DIDN'T LOOK RIGHT

Bobby Karras was seventeen years old and he was walking to work. The weather was nice, so why not? Backpack slung over his right shoulder.

He worked for his older brother. His parents were dead. They'd been old when Bobby was born, so Tad Karras was more like a father than an older brother, but Bobby didn't want any of that *Father Knows Best* stuff from Tad.

Bobby didn't even plan to work for his brother that much longer. He'd read you could get a degree in racetrack management out in the west somewhere and so he was thinking about that. He had the horseshoe ring on, the one belonging to his father. Tad said he could go ahead and have it.

Tad didn't want to talk about their parents. He didn't want to talk about the years they had lived on the little island. Tad didn't want to talk about the old life. He barely even wanted to speak in their native language even though his English wasn't as good as Bobby's.

"Live for today, Bobby," Tad said. "Don't look

back. That's for your losers."

Then Tad would give Bobby the look.

Tad said Bobby had been too young to remember what things had been like on Symi. What things had really been like.

Tad didn't want to talk about what had happened on Symi.

Somehow, though, Bobby was going to go back there.

In his dreams he saw the windmills on the hill overlooking the beach. He had played there, running in and out of them and climbing the rocks around them. One of Odysseus's men.

And like Odysseus's men, he knew he would return some day to the island.

Right now, though, it was only a dream. Like the song Tad liked.

Only Make Believe.

He wasn't like his brother. Tad was content to look at the picture of their old home.

Bobby wanted to go back. Find his relatives.

He was going to do it, and he was going to do it a hell of a lot sooner than Tad.

❊ ❊ ❊

Bobby was coming into the diner early today.

Bobby hoped Iris was there and Tad was not. Tad liked to boss Bobby around when Iris was there. Bobby figured Tad had a thing for Iris. Who wouldn't?

Tad just didn't have the guts do something about it.

Bobby knew Iris liked him. She kidded Bobby, but she was nice about it.

He'd kissed her a couple of times and she didn't mind that too much at all.

Bobby just figured he had to wait until the time was right.

✽ ✽ ✽

The Gremlin was parked in front. Maybe he could grab it later. Take Iris to the beach.

Something was wrong. Bobby knew it.

He stood outside the front door. There was music blaring loud from the jukebox. Not the kind of music Tad liked, either.

It didn't look right.

He walked around to the back entrance. The doors in the alley led into the kitchen. Bobby knew where his brother kept the key.

He opened the back door as quietly as he could.

HOWARD JOHNSON'S

Lefty drove north.

He was able to pick up the pace a little in the Winnebago but not too much.

He was getting hungry when he started seeing signs for Howard Johnson's.

This HoJo's was pretty much the same as the one in Bangor where Lefty had eaten plenty of times.

He would order fried clams in Maine any time, but he wouldn't eat them this far south.

He would wait until he got home.

Lefty was hungry though, so he turned the Winnebago into the parking lot of the Howard Johnson's.

He looked over the menu while the waitress stood next to his table. She'd shown him in and parked him near the kitchen and the cigarette machine. He had a good view of the peaked orange roof of the motor lodge.

"Cheeseburger with French fries," Lefty said. "Gravy over the spuds. HoJo Cola."

The waitress nodded.

Lefty glanced at the kitchen, seeing an older man in a white T-shirt standing behind the grill. Maybe Howard Johnson himself.

A group of three teenagers, two boys and a girl came in making noise.

"Gravy over the spuds," the waitress repeated Lefty's order like she heard it every day. Paying no attention to the teenagers who had seated themselves near Lefty.

"I like them that way too," she said.

Her nametag identified her as Debbie.

"Thanks, Debbie,"

Debbie smiled. "Coming right up."

* * *

The teenagers were laughing, joking and the two boys were taking turns hitting each other. One of the boys started to make fart noises. The girl was singing a Peter, Paul and Mary song badly.

They couldn't see Lefty, but he could see him.

The cheeseburger did the trick and the gravy fries were good.

"You like that?" Debbie said.

Lefty nodded. He was watching the kids in the back booth. They were eating sundaes. Big ones. The one boy had shifted from fart noises to long belches.

The girl thought it was hysterical.

"Do it again, Ronnie," she said.

Ronnie did it again.

Lefty slipped two ten dollar bills under the glass of cold water. That would cover his lunch and a healthy tip for Debbie. She'd earned it.

The teenagers were quiet.

Like they said in the movies, they were too quiet. Conspiratorial.

Debbie was behind the counter walking back to the kitchen.

* * *

Lefty caught up to the kids before they were able to jam back into their VW. Just as he'd predicted, the girl had gone first, then the two boys bolted for the door.

* * *

In the parking lot, Lefty grabbed the taller boy by the collar of his maroon striped rugby shirt. Yanked the collar back, spinning the kid into his buddy. The collision knocked the wind out of the second one, who lay on the ground holding his stomach. Lefty pulled him up. Holding both of them by their hair, Lefty slammed their foreheads together and pushed them against the rear of the

Volkswagen.

The girl was screaming. Calling Lefty a pig.

"Shut up," Lefty said.

He turned back to the boys. They were perched next to the bumper sticker on the Volkswagen reading *QUESTION AUTHORITY*.

Lefty held the taller kid's face up.

"You didn't pay, Ronnie. You need to go back and do that."

Ronnie mumbled something and the girl whined.

Lefty turned.

"I thought I told you to shut up."

He looked at the two boys.

"Which one of you has money?"

The shorter boy slowly lifted his hand.

"I got some money," he said.

"Get in there and pay her. Once she raises her hand gives me the thumbs up, I'll let you go on your way. No funny stuff. Ten percent tip."

※ ※ ※

Debbie looked out of the plate glass window of the Howard Johnson's.

Lefty saw her looking at him and the two kids next to the VW.

She raised her hand, then gave him the sign with her thumb. She kept waving even after the shorter boy came back out.

The kids got into the Volkswagen, the girl giving Lefty the finger from the back seat.

They pulled out onto the highway.

Lefty watched them go. Saw the route they were taking. Not heading on the highway. Local kids.

He walked back to the Winnebago.

The air was still and Lefty felt the heaviness of the humidity and the rising summer temperature.

THE POOL CUE

Iris saw a shadow from across the room. She used her will to not follow the shadow. She couldn't let Max see what was approaching.

Iris kept moving her hips to the rhythm of the record, hoping she would distract Max.

She lifted one finger toward Max's eyes, directing him downward toward her now open blouse.

Look up here, she wanted to say. Look up here at me, Max, from out of the pools of your Schlitz malt liquor and do not look behind you.

She willed herself not to look between Max and the lifeless body of Tad Karras at the shadow which had now taken real form between the two rows of booths.

Bobby Karras stood poised.

Bobby, seventeen years old, holding the skinny end of a pool cue with both hands and bringing it back like Jimmy Connors in the split second before he would deliver a serve.

The fat end of the stick rushed downward and smashed the top of Max's skull like the concave surface of a teaspoon splitting a soft boiled egg.

Max toppled like a rag doll in front of Iris and blood spilled over his face and eyes.

Iris ran to Bobby.

"Oh my God," she said. She kissed him hard on the lips.

Bobby looked around the room. Max was out cold. He grabbed Max's gun from the booth next to the jukebox.

"No, Bobby," Iris said.

Bobby pointed the gun at Max's head for a long five seconds.

Iris watched. It felt like an eternity to her.

Bobby dropped the gun down to waist level, then looked at the leather bag near Max.

"I'll put it in here," he said.

She couldn't speak. She watched Bobby unzip the bag and put the gun in the top.

"Hold this," he said. He handed her the bag. "His car's out back where I came in. You wanna help me with this guy?"

"What are you doing, Bobby," Iris said.

Bobby was fidgeting with the leather bag and then he looked down at Max.

"Grab his shoulder," Bobby said. He had started to drag Max away from the jukebox.

Dragging him wasn't difficult, Max wasn't putting up any resistance with the dent Bobby had put in the side of his head. That cue stick was heavy.

Max wasn't heavy though. Iris looked at him in a different way from the way she'd usually seen him. Instead of the leering psychopath, Iris saw Max was a smallish guy wearing clothes too small even for him.

Bobby stopped dragging Max for a second and looked over at Iris. Max's body looked lifeless.

"Get his pockets, wouldja, Iris?"

Iris squinted and shook her head.

"What are you talking about," Bobby?"

"See what's in them."

Iris gave Max's pockets a desultory pat.

"No," Bobby said. "Really check them."

Iris gave a tentative poke, pulled a BIC lighter out of Max's pants pockets.

"Go all down his body, Iris. Even his boots."

Max wore white vinyl boots with zippers. Elevator heels on the boots maybe giving an extra two inches over sea level. Iris found a small chrome automatic in Max's right boot. Held it up.

"I don't get this, Bobby," she said. "I don't get this at all."

"Put that in the bag, too."

Bobby kicked the swinging door to the kitchen, dragged Max in, held a napkin over his hand, opened the door to the walk-in cooler, pulled Max inside completely, then slammed the heavy brushed aluminum door shut with his elbow.

"He can't get out of there," Bobby said. "That's gonna give us some time to think."

"And call the cops, right?" Iris said. "He killed Tad."

"You didn't see that," Bobby said. "All you saw

was a drunk guy holding a gun."

"Oh my God," she said. "What are you talking about, Bobby?"

"You weren't here," he said. "Neither of us was here."

Bobby grabbed the leather bag. Picked up his own backpack. He pulled Iris along with him around the corner to the front door.

"Don't touch anything else, Iris," Bobby said. "We weren't here."

ON ICE

Inside the walk-in cooler, Max Hellman started to come out of the dark emptiness caused by the concussion. He lay in darkness, wondering where he was and how long he had been lying here.

He could nearly reconstruct everything from the time he first saw Tad and the leather bag, to watching Iris dance in front of the jukebox.

Then nothing.

A curtain had dropped after which he remembered nothing.

His head was killing him.

He knew Tad hadn't hit him. By the time Tad figured out what was going on, the best he'd been able to do was to lunge for the bag. Too late.

Max enjoyed remembering Tad's panic, but his head hurt too badly for him to appreciate it fully.

Tad thought he was some kind of wiseguy, handling all that bread every week.

Iris coming in had been unexpected.

She really knew how to put on a show. She had been in front of him the whole time so it couldn't have been her.

And it couldn't have been Al.

Al was on Max's side no matter what. Al had done whatever Max wanted him to do ever since they'd been kids running the streets of Rumford and Mexico, Maine.

They did everything together. Max remembered showing Al how to shoplift. Al had gotten pretty good. He'd only gotten caught a couple of times and those were when he'd forgotten what Max had told him.

They'd stolen a couple of cars together and gotten tattoos on the same day at Old Orchard Beach. Max had gotten a skull with a dagger and snake. Al chose Tweety Bird. Al had even gotten Max the job here at the Taverna Frigging Athena. The job had turned out to be a zero, but without the job Max would have never have figured out about Tad's cash and then this whole thing wouldn't have happened.

Max tried to look around in the dark, but couldn't make anything out. He couldn't even see his hand when he held it in front of his face.

This whole thing *had* happened, but it hadn't worked out the way Max planned it.

At least it hadn't so far.

Max was cold and cooped up.

It felt like the winter months in Rumford when he'd been a kid. Max remembered lying in bed next to a window covered with frost, holding his finger on the window to watch the ice melt.

This place was just as cold, but now Max could barely move. His body was cramped in a confined space on freezing concrete. Max felt like he was lying on a sheet of ice. There was no room on either side of Max. Max couldn't extend his arms. He could only move them up, but his head ached like he had the worst hangover he could ever imagine.

He knew who had done it. There was only one person who could have knocked Max out. Bobby didn't know Max was going to be there. Bobby was so dumb he didn't even know how dumb he was. Bobby was one of those dumb guys who thinks they're smart.

Max smelled onions. Onions and mildew.

With the force of his will, Max worked himself upright. The area inside the cooler was dark, cold and claustrophobic. It felt like he had been buried alive.

Bobby probably figured he was entitled to the money in the bag, on account of it having come from his brother. Max shook his head. He wouldn't let Bobby get the money. It was one thing for Bobby to knock Max out and drag him into a walk-in cooler. It was another thing to steal Max's money. Bobby should have known better than that. If he didn't, Max would have to teach him a lesson.

Max worked his hand up to his shirt pocket and felt around for a cigarette. The damp front of his shirt distracted him. Max felt the slick polyester fabric and the liquid. Brought his fingers from his nose to his lips. Tasted his own blood. Moved his hand to his head and felt the dent where the pain came from. He felt the blood congealed on his scalp.

He was able to stick his other hand in his pants pocket far enough to bring out his BIC lighter. Max flicked the wheel, adjusted the flame, then looked around.

The walk in cooler was big enough to hold him, but just barely. In front of him were doors he knew would not open, and on each side of him were shelves of vegetables, blocks of cheese and white plastic containers of who-knows-what. He reached in his shirt pocket again, and in the bottom of pack of cigarettes Max found a joint he'd put in earlier in the day.

He saw a couple cases of Narragansetts.

Not his favorite, but what the hell, it was something.

He flicked the lighter again. He would need to conserve fuel, he supposed. Right now, he needed to think about his situation.

He pushed on the door then banged against it, knowing he wouldn't be able to get out.

He took a long drag on the joint and held the smoke in his lungs.

He was going to have to think.

Sit tight and think.

PISCATAQUA BRIDGE

After crossing the six lane Piscataqua Bridge into Kittery, Maine, Lefty left Interstate 95 and started north on Route 1.

He would lose time, but Route 1 was the best way to travel the length of Maine's coast.

He thought about stopping for his first lobster roll of the season at Red's Eats in Wiscasset. They were famous, but he'd never bothered going there and braving the line.

That wasn't too far ahead on Route 1.

Maybe today.

There were a lot of good diners in the Portland area, particularly in South Portland. Lefty knew he could get a good breakfast in any of them.

As usual, traffic in the city was congested.

Lefty decided to keep moving and avoid the hubbub of the city.

RUNNING WITH THE DEVIL

"You're thinking I should call the cops?" Bobby said.

They were driving north on Route 1 in Tad's car, a dark blue Cadillac Fleetwood Brougham. Iris was looking in the mirror in the visor of the passenger seat. The ocean was to the right, but Iris wasn't paying attention to the view. The brown leather getaway bag lay in front of the back seats.

Bobby had turned the air conditioner on high and was obeying the speed limit just as if he was taking Tad's car out for a morning spin. Iris had seen him going through Tad's pockets.

She had wanted to turn away, not look at him doing it. It felt like Bobby was taking the coins from a dead man's eyes. Bobby had taken Tad's keys with the silver Greek letters. Probably the same ones on his cufflinks.

Tad had left the Mantovani tape in the cassette this morning. Maybe the last music he'd ever heard, Iris thought.

A Summer Place. She remembered watching

Sandra Dee and Troy Donahue when the movie had been on *Saturday Night at the Movies*, years before. It had been filmed on the coast of Maine and here they were, driving up the coast themselves.

Bobby was trying hard not to look too nervous. He listened to the Mantovani for less than a minute before popping the tape out and switching to a rock station broadcasting out of Bangor.

Van Halen.

Running With the Devil.

* * *

Iris remembered Tad explaining the difference between the regular Fleetwood and the Fleetwood Brougham to Bobby.

"Detroit's going to mess the Cadillac up, you watch," Tad had said. "That's why I got the Brougham. Everything's going to be all about gas miles cause of the Arabs. Guy I know says they might go with front wheel drive, too. Might as well drive a Jap car at that point. I mean, where's it gonna end?"

* * *

"I don't know, Bobby," Iris said. "I don't know

anything. Why are we running away? Why not call the police. Maybe I just don't get any of this."

Bobby shook his head. "My brother's dead on the floor back there."   He pounded the steering wheel. "Son-of-a-bitch shot him. I should have just gone ahead and finished him off. I should have turned around and shot him in the middle of his miserable head."

Iris shook her head. "No, Bobby. You did the right thing. You want to go to prison, or what?"

Bobby's face betrayed no emotion. He looked over at her.

"Prison?" Bobby said. "You think I'm worried about going to prison? You know what's in the bag?"

"There's two guns in the bag. I know that. I put one of them in there," she said. "You saw me do it."

Bobby shrugged his head toward the back seat.

"Look in it, wouldja? Look under the guns. Just take a damn look."

"I don't want to take a look, Bobby. I don't want anything to do with this. Whatever it is."

She pulled a cigarette from her purse. Looked around for matches but didn't find any. She found the lighter on the wood paneled dashboard of the Cadillac and punched it in.

"Do it," he said. "Just so you know what we're dealing with."

"What are you talking about, Bobby. Tell me."

"Prison's nothing compared to what these guys would do to me, Iris. That's what I'm talking about."

Iris turned around in the leather passenger seat. Looked at the brown bag on the floor of the back seat.

"Pull it up," Bobby said. "Look in it."

Iris put her knees onto the passenger seat and leaned over into the back of the car. Facing the back window she felt disoriented and off-balance. She pulled the overnight bag up by the handle. Placing it on the rear seat, she unzipped the bag. The two guns were different sizes. The gun Max had held was much larger than the one she'd found in his boot. Beneath the guns was a Portland newspaper with a picture of a marching band practicing for the Fourth of July. She looked under the paper. There were rows of bills. Ten dollar bills, twenty dollar bills. All of them neatly banded and stacked.

She zipped the bag and returned it gently to the place on the floor of the car where it had been.

Iris turned back around and sat back in her seat.

She put her safety belt on again.

"It's a problem, Iris," Bobby said. "First problem is, Max is gonna survive. His head's too thick for that pool cue to kill him. Count on that. I just knocked him out. Second problem is if he or Al finds us."

"I need to get out of this car, Bobby," Iris said. "I don't need this. I don't need any of this."

Bobby shook his head. He was pushing down harder on the accelerator.

"That's a problem too, Iris." Bobby turned and faced her. His features were more delicate than those of Tad. They really didn't look like brothers.

"I'm not kidding, Bobby. I want to get out."

The scenery was going by more quickly. The road was empty in front of them. Next month, the traffic would slow down into the twenties through here.

"It's a big problem for you, Iris. You say you don't need any of this? Listen, you already got this. Max and Al both know who you are. And they know what you saw."

Bobby pointed his thumb over his shoulder at the bag.

"Police are the least of our problems. Those guys are gonna want their cash back."

"Max and Al?"

Bobby shook his head.

"Who's money is it, Bobby?"

"What difference does that make?" Bobby said. "We got it, and they're going to want it back. You wanna bring the cops into it, we end up dead. And who keeps the money?"

"You tell me, Bobby," she said.

He was clutching the wheel with hands turning white.

"Tell me what your great plan is," Iris said. "Just tell me about it."

SPACE INVADERS

Al LeBlanc didn't like getting too uptight about how long Max was out of their shared apartment. Al knew Max as well as anybody, they'd grown up down the street from each other in Rumford.

Max had his own way of doing a job, and this wasn't any big deal.

In fact, Al wouldn't have noticed Max's absence if he hadn't managed to rack up a record score on *Space Invaders*. He wanted to show Max the score, but Max wasn't around.

You could just look around to see who was in the apartment over the hardware store.

Al had looked around the place, checking out Max's part of the apartment and even under the covers of the bed he slept in. Sometimes Max left his dirty laundry knotted under the sheets, making it looked like he was still in bed.

Then Al remembered.

Max had said he was going to Tad's place even though they weren't working today. Then Max had said something in a hurry and Al hadn't heard him because he was involved in the game of *Space Invaders*. Something about some money.

Al hoped Max would remember to bring back some chicken wings from the Taverna Athena. He was starting to get hungry. Al blinked his eyes and stood up from the television.

The *Space Invaders* were now coming down in a freefall and he really didn't care at this point. It was almost time to move on to another game anyway.

It just didn't feel the same when you didn't have to shell out money to play the game. After a while, continuing with the game just felt like work. It was like when Al worked at the discount shoe store. He didn't have much to do at the place except wait for a pneumatic tube to come down and then he'd have to bring up shoes from the back. Chris Summerfield, who worked at the warehouse told him about the phone in the office nobody watched. You could make long distance calls on that phone for as long as you wanted. Problem was, Al didn't have anybody he wanted to call long-distance. He'd made a couple long-distance calls to the other side of the country just for the hell of it, but he got sick of that pretty quick. If Max was there, it would have been more fun. Max would have had someone to call.

Max said that's why they needed to change games again. They were pretty much done with *Space Invaders* like they were already done with *Pacman*. Al was glad Max was also finished with *Pong*. Al remembered Max playing that game for hours with the control in one hand and a joint in the other. Max never had gotten sick of watching that little white dot go from one side of the screen to the other.

Max probably wouldn't be back any time soon.

Al decided to take advantage of his roommate's absence. Thumbing through the stack of albums next to the tower holding Max's stereo, Al took out the Brother's Johnson album.

Strawberry Letter 23.

Made a minute adjustment to the graphic equalizer and blasted the speakers.

Al loved the song almost as much as Max hated it.

Al reached under the orange floral patterned couch and pulled out the ice tray. He rolled a joint with paper from the orange Zig Zag package then paused to admire his handiwork before lighting the joint with a gold-tipped match from the Taverna Athena.

Looking around, Al saw Max still hadn't gotten back. Al was hungry, but he knew there wasn't much in the kitchen except some peanut butter and a loaf of Nissen Canadian White bread he'd gotten half price at the A&P.

Max was probably down at the Taverna. Probably eating something without giving Al a second thought.

Al thought about walking to the Taverna. If they weren't too busy, Tad would make him something and take it off his next paycheck. Really, Al suspected Tad didn't even do that. He'd never shorted one of Al's checks. Tad was a good guy.

Tad would fix him up with some souvlaki or something. That would definitely be better than peanut butter.

He knew better than to call Tad though. Tying up the phone at the Taverna pissed Tad off.

Al stood up. Put the ice cube tray back on the floor then slid it under with the heel of his boot.

He was a little pissed Max hadn't come back.

FROM THE DINER
IN EASTPORT

"It's getting dark, Bobby."

"They'll kill you, Iris. Either one of them. Al doesn't know what's going on half the time, but he'll do anything Max tells him to do. And you know about Max now. He'd kill you soon as look at you."

Iris knew Bobby was telling the truth, and that was why she hadn't gotten out of the car, even when she could have. She was scared for herself and also for Bobby, who didn't look like he had any kind of a plan.

"What do you think I should do, Iris? You think I should call the cops? What's gonna happen to the money?"

"Throw the money into the water," Iris said.

She pointed at the water of the bay on the right hand of the car. Bobby was driving the speed limit.

"Next bridge, just throw that thing out."

"No way," Bobby said. He shook his head. "No point in that."

That was when Iris decided to tell Bobby about

Lefty.

* * *

"You know this guy," Bobby said. "What does that even mean? I mean you're all like 'I know this guy.' How's some guy you barely know going to help?"

The truth was, Iris didn't know if Lefty could help Bobby.

But she knew Lefty would help her.

* * *

She'd never met anyone like Lefty.

The whole scene had been like something out of one of those western movies her brother liked watching. Iris had to admit, she liked watching them too, especially the ones with Clint Eastwood.

Iris would have never guessed Lefty, the guy sitting in the back of the diner wearing khakis and a flannel shirt was more than a match for the two outlaw bikers.

She had barely even noticed him sitting in the place. Lefty was a pretty average looking guy.

The two guys in the gang colors were messing with her. Green Hornets Motorcycle Club from Skowhegan. Somehow, they'd gotten her into the corner of the diner. This time of day, she was the only one in the front of the diner, and Barney, the cook was pretty much deaf and helpless. Nobody else would be able to hear Iris if she screamed.

Big green hornets were stitched across the backs of their denim jacket. Greasy hair and dirty down to the fingers.

They'd waited until she was alone.

She didn't know why they were here, so far from Skowhegan.

The guy missing his front tooth had put his hand up the front of her apron, under the skirt she was required to wear.

The other one, the one with pig eyes looked around.

Either he didn't notice Lefty, or he didn't consider him anyone he needed to worry about.

❊ ❊ ❊

What happened next, happened quickly.

Lefty came out of the booth where he'd been sitting. He'd seen everything.

He held his gun in front of himself, somehow managing to keep it on both the men.

Then Lefty had barked some orders.

Lefty grabbed both bikers and smashed their foreheads together with a sickening intensity.

Then, he'd walked them out of the place, a guy who only minutes before had been sitting in the back booth finishing his clam roll.

＊　＊　＊

Iris looked at Bobby.

"I don't know what he can do, Bobby, I just know him from the diner in Eastport. From back when I worked up there." She looked at Bobby. "You can drop me off there."

Bobby shook his head.

"This guy's what, Dudley Do-Right?"

"I don't know, Bobby, I just want out. His sister's got a place where she rents rooms. I can stay there."

＊　＊　＊

After Lefty took the bikers outside, Iris heard the roar of the big motorcycles.

She listened to them leaving and watched Lefty come back in the place and sit back down with his clam roll.

"Got some more tartar sauce for these?" he had said.

She had brought the tartar sauce in the little paper cups. Two of them. Sat down across from Lefty in the booth. Put her head back against the back of the booth.

"I don't know what to say," she had said.

"They won't be back," Lefty had said. "I'll stick

around for a while, but you won't be seeing them. They're gone."

Something about the way he said it made her know he was telling the truth.

Lefty had come back a couple of times. They had talked a lot. He had told her some funny stories about the place in Cutler and a few of his baseball stories.

She told him about her dream of going to the little town south of Myrtle Beach. Starting a place of her own there. The place was just a funky little beach town where everyone knew everyone. Like Mayberry, maybe. Lefty had laughed and said all those places were like Mayberry until you got to know them.

Then he'd stopped, when he saw she was serious.

"Hey, if that's your dream, why not do it?" he had said.

He told her how she could get in touch with him and what she needed to do if they came back.

"I don't think they're coming back, but if you're by yourself, nothing wrong with closing up shop you hear those bikes out on the street. Those boys don't like going anywhere without advertising their arrival, do they?"

She had shook her head.

"Just close the place up. Lock it from the inside and leave out the back. Thing is, though, I doubt they come back."

On his second trip back to the diner he'd

brought her something.

He brought Iris a gun. Small, but not a toy. A man-stopper.

He'd shown her how to use it out in a clearing out in the woods. He'd worked with her until he was confident she knew what she was doing.

"It's a tool," Lefty had said. "You remember *Shane*, don't you? A gun's only as good as the person holding it, right?"

"What did you say to them," she said. "How do you know they won't be back?"

Lefty hadn't answered directly, just shook his head.

She missed him when he stopped dropping in, but he'd told her she could always count on him if she was in trouble.

* * *

Bobby was ready to stop. Iris could tell he was starting to get road weary. She knew what it felt like. Bobby was starting to have problems driving.

"We gotta stop somewhere, I guess. This guy, what's his name?" Bobby said, "he better not ask a lot of questions. And he sure as hell can't know about the money."

"He won't know anything you don't tell him, Bobby," Iris said. "I'm not going to say anything."

Bobby drove on in silence. They were close to Machias, where they would need to turn to get out to Cutler.

"Tell me about this place, Iris," Bobby said "What's it look like out there?"

*　*　*

Lefty had described Cutler and the Little River Island to Iris.

"It's not much of a place," Lefty had said.

He had told her about Cutler, the little town where he lived. Compared to Cutler, Houlton was a big city.

"It's one road in and one road out. There's lobster boats going out in the morning and coming back at night. There's an island at the mouth of the bay with a lighthouse and even that's deactivated."

"What's that mean it's deactivated? They just let boats crash on the rocks now?"

Lefty had shook his head.

"It's a big island. The light's outdated so they have an electronic one on a timer. Nobody's out there."

"I'd like to go there, sometime," Iris said.

"Maybe I could take you there if you get a free day."

*　*　*

"Nobody?" Bobby said. "There's nobody on the island? No Coast Guard? Nothing?"

Bobby looked interested now.

"How big's this island?"

"Let me spell something out for you, Bobby."

She turned and faced him.

Bobby continued driving, staring at the winding road in front of him.

"I want you to leave me at Lefty's," Iris said. "I'll be safe, if it's me you're worried about. You can do what you need to do. I won't say another word. As far as I'm concerned, none of this happened. You're on your own, though."

"You say anything, Iris, it's not me you gotta worry about."

* * *

Lefty took Iris out to the island once.

Lefty had taken her to the Inn. *Gallagher's Summer Place Inn* the sign out front said. His sister hadn't been there and Lefty had been glad about that.

Lefty had shown her the wharf and the little beach in town where he told her she could find sea glass.

She found a few pieces. White, blue, green. Beautiful.

Ricky Dunbar had been on his way out to

the bird island that day. Lefty laughed about the birdwatchers who sometimes came to the inn, single-minded in their pursuit of seabirds. Lefty said he liked birds, but he personally wasn't a damn fool about them.

They took Lefty's runabout to the island. The Mercury pushed the boat through the water nicely. It was different from lakes up north. More choppy than either Grand or Drew's Lake where she'd gone with her friends to their family camps. Lefty gave her the tiller for a while. He pointed at the island at the mouth of the bay.

"Can't miss it, can you?" he had said.

He grilled two lobsters on the beach and then they stayed on the beach until it was starting to get dark.

Iris remembered it as a perfect day.

✻ ✻ ✻

Iris watched the road.

Bobby was kind of a bad driver, accelerating the Cadillac in time with whatever song was on the radio. The big car was supposed to be smooth, but not when Bobby was driving. She was thinking about Lefty, who would at least be able to deal with Bobby.

She could tell Lefty everything from the start of the day. Since she came in and saw Tad shot dead.

She didn't know what else to do.

Bobby's plan was no plan.

Iris knew the longer she stayed with Bobby, the more dangerous everything would become for her.

And it was getting late.

Bobby turned toward Iris. His smile didn't look the same now.

"I been thinking about it, Iris." He took his right hand off the steering wheel and patted her shoulder.

"I'll take you there," he said.

Iris breathed.

"I might be able to work something out. Just don't say anything to this guy," he said. "Let me do the talking."

BASEBALL MONEY

Lefty Gallagher made a left hand turn into Gallagher's Summer Place Inn in Cutler, Maine.

Just a little more than fifteen hundred miles, and he'd made it to home sweet home for the summer months.

Fifty degrees in Cutler compared to humid nineties, the lupine out the window of the Winnebago, Cutler was paradise after the last few weeks in Florida.

Five o'clock in the afternoon. This far north there was still plenty of sunshine. Lefty would get a good look at the town before actually stopping at the inn.

Gallagher's Summer Place Inn was Lefty's sister's place. Back when he still had baseball money coming in, Lefty had bought the place with cash a few years ago and given Olive a lifetime half-interest. Lefty recognized now he'd been influenced by nostalgia, but nevertheless, he enjoyed the peace and quiet.

Lefty and Olive had both grown up in Cutler,

but neither had lived there for many years. Lefty had his baseball career and Olive had been a teacher before she retired, supporting her alcoholic husband Ernie until his death a few years before.

Lefty made some money during his career, but not as much as he he could have if he'd started in baseball just ten or twelve years later.

He'd started his career before free-agency could have brought him more money and he'd retired before steroids   could have kept him in the game longer.

Olive wanted to name it *A Summer Place* after the movie which had taken place on an island on the coast of Maine.

Lefty had put his foot down. They had worked out a compromise which Lefty was happy with.

Gallagher's Summer Place Inn in Cutler.

The name just barely fit on the sign.

Lefty planned to take a look around the Inn to see what progress his sister had made in the last couple of weeks. Then he could see what he would need to do himself.

Olive would open the place for the summer season in a week or so. She was busy this time of year, airing out the rooms and making them ready for guests.

Last summer, Lefty had painted the big sign which hung in front of the Summer Place Inn. The green and gold lettering on the white sign sparkled when hit by the sun.

Everything on the coast of Maine looked good in June.

Olive was ready for guests to arrive. She had unhooked the small *NO VACANCIES* sign hanging beneath the big sign and replaced it with another one.

TRANSIENTS WELCOME - EUROPEAN PLAN.

European Plan, Olive had explained to Lefty years before meant she didn't provide any meals.

"Why do you say that when you give them breakfast?" Lefty said.

"It sounds better," Olive said. "It's more sophisticated. Plus, it makes them feel as if they are getting something extra when I serve them breakfast."

This sign would stay up all summer, because there were never nights where the inn was completely full.

Olive insisted on the part of the sign welcoming transients even though Lefty had told her the wording implied she was advertising rooms for vagrants.

"I'm perfectly familiar with the expanded meaning of that word, Arthur," she said, "but the sign has always been worded thus. Probably since the turn of the century."

Lefty's sister Olive kept Lefty's room available for his exclusive use. In return, Lefty scraped and painted the place before the arrival of the tourists, put screens in the windows, and performed odd jobs.

Walter P. Jennings, wearing his yellow mesh ball cap, stood in his front yard next to the inn. He was waving his garden hose across a stack of lobster traps.

Lefty slowed down and rolled his window down.

"Looking for work?" Walter said.

"Not hardly," Lefty said, "I'm sure Olive's got plenty to keep me busy."

He honked his horn to warn Olive of his arrival before making his turn into the Summer Place Inn.

Olive was here, but Lefty couldn't see her.

She had been busy over the winter.

Things had changed in the Inn in a way Lefty did not expect.

The velvet love seat had been pulled to the other side of the room. Despite its rock-hard horsehair upholstery, the love seat was Lefty's favorite place to read old Saturday Evening Posts before his afternoon nap. The magazines were all at least forty years old. Some of them had Norman Rockwell covers and dated from World War II. Lefty enjoyed the advertisements for cars, cigarettes, and razor blades in those magazines. Occasionally, Lefty would buy more magazines at the Antique Attic in Harrington. Along with Reader's Digest Condensed Books, Lefty was well stocked with reading material.

He would have preferred for Olive to leave the love seat and the stack of magazines alone next to the bay window. Moving the love seat made the place feel less like home.

In place of the love seat, Olive had dragged a pair of uncomfortable rockers.

She'd even moved the oar.

The ten foot Shaw and Tenney oar from FDR's estate on Campobello Island was one of Lefty's prized possessions and the centerpiece of the Inn's living room.

Lefty had painted the oar forest green long ago and put it over the sofa.

He looked around and the oar was nowhere to be seen. His prized Robin Hood Toby mug stood on the marble topped table in the entry. Olive had taken it from his room over the winter and filled it with flowers. Something that looked like Dutchman's breeches, but probably weren't. Lefty remembered Walter P. Jennings, in one of the monologues he used to indulge in, saying the original species had been considered a cure for syphilis by the Abenaki.

"Hi, Olive," Lefty said.

Olive had come downstairs wearing a hooded sweatshirt over tights. She was holding a hammer as if she had been mid-project when she heard the Winnebago pull into the driveway.

Lefty took his Robin Hood Toby mug and carefully placed it on the bookshelf where it belonged, face to the wall.

The stereo was playing.

Olive loved listening to her record collection while working in the rooms.

Olive's look was quizzical, as if she was having a hard time placing Lefty.

"How was your season?" she said.

Carole King was singing *So Far Away.*

"I've been in Daytona Beach, remember?" Lefty said. He waved at her. "I'm your brother."

"I know exactly who you are, Arthur," she said. "Don't be so dense. I put that paddle in the carriage house, where it belongs. Your mail's on the table. And no, I haven't looked at it."

Arthur.

A minor irritation. He'd made it clear to Olive she should call him Lefty, but she rarely did.

Nevertheless, Lefty was his name.

Lefty Gallagher.

Nobody called him Arthur anymore, except Olive.

"It's not a paddle, Olive," Lefty said. "It's an oar, and it's a piece of history."

Lefty left the mail on the marble topped table.

"I'm glad you're home, Arthur," Olive said.

FLEETWOOD BROUGHAM

"So, you're telling me Tad worked with the mob." Iris had opened the passenger side window of the Fleetwood Brougham. She tapped the ashes from her cigarette out onto Route 1.

"It's not exactly like that, Iris," Bobby said. "He'd do a favor here and there and he'd get a favor in return. That's how the world goes around, isn't it?"

They had passed Rockland, Rockport, Camden. The midday sun was overhead. Iris had thought about getting out of the car in Camden. It would have been easy, maybe tell Bobby she wanted to get something for lunch at French and Brawn and slip out the back of the place. She could have lost him in Camden easily. But now he was saying he'd get her to Cutler. Leave her with Lefty. At least Lefty would know what to do. She'd be safe with him.

"Sure Bobby," Iris said. "I've seen the movies. I just didn't figure Tad for the type."

She knew Bobby was right. Whatever had happened to Tad, Iris was involved with it now.

Max scared her and Bobby was beginning to

scare her also.

"What about you, Bobby?" Iris was angry. She pointed at the bag of money. "Guns and money, right? You knew about this, didn't you?"

"Not me, Iris," he said. "I just came in to work today. Tad didn't want me involved. He kept saying I'm his little brother, so he was going to shield me from that part of the business."

"Max and Al," she said. "Those guys and Tad?"

"No way," Bobby said. He shook his head. "You might as well be talking about the Three Stooges, you're talking about those two. Plus, there's no way Tad would ever have gotten involved with Max. Max is nuts."

Bobby shook his head.

"I went to the place those guys lived once. Tad would've killed me. Over a hardware store in Saco. They drink, smoke dope and play this game they got hooked up to a black and white TV. They sit there for hours playing Ms Pacman, Space Invaders, things like that. That's their thing."

"What about you?"

Bobby lifted his hands from the wheel.

"Look at me. My hands are clean, Iris," he said. "You saw me. I guess that's why I didn't kill him. I want to stay clean."

She looked out on the road ahead. The white clapboard houses sparkled in the early summer sun and the coast was bathed in a warm glow. The houses looked different during the long winter months when dark days conspired with cold and damp weather.

She glanced again behind her seat.

Bobby might think his hands were clean, but the brown leather bag he'd thrown back there was dirty.

She wondered if she was part of this, like Bobby said.

KNUCKLEBALL SPECIALIST

Though he was right-handed, Lefty felt the name Lefty suited him better than the name Arthur. Being called 'Arthur' made Lefty feel uncomfortable.

Even though his name was Lefty, he had always thrown with his right hand and batted from the right side of the plate until sophomore year in high school when he had fallen out of a tree trying to get a better view of Danae Jennings sunbathing in her back yard.

Something funny happened to his arm in the healing process. Doctors later said it had to do with his tendons. The accident turned Lefty into a pitcher.

Not just a pitcher, but a very successful one.

And the accident gave him the name 'Lefty.'

He told people he should have been written up in the medical journals.

Tommy John had a surgical procedure named after him, and Tommy John couldn't do what Lefty learned to do.

Lefty Gallagher had spent the rest of that season and the summer, learning to pitch and hit as a lefty.

When his arm healed, he went back to using his right arm, mostly, but he found his left arm had essentially the same strength and coordination as his right.

People had started calling him Lefty, and he liked the name.

Lefty was signed out of high school as a right handed pitcher. When he lost a notch on his fastball, he returned to the knuckleball, a pitch he'd learned as a kid from none other than Walter P. Jennings.

Jennings claimed to have learned the pitch from Eddie Cicotte himself, while the notorious White Sox pitcher was barnstorming under an assumed name following the Black Sox scandal.

Lefty pitched many more innings as a knuckleball specialist than he ever pitched with his fastball.

He pitched for over a dozen years in the minor leagues with occasional call-ups to the bigs in Cleveland, Detroit, Oakland, and Montreal.

For a while, Lefty enjoyed a speaking career at lodge meetings and little league events.

"Call me Lefty," he would always say when speaking at banquets. "Whoever heard of a pitcher named Righty?"

Once in a while, a smart-aleck would challenge the assertion.

The first time it happened, it caught Lefty unprepared.

A guy at a Elks Club banquet decided to get wise.

After the usual introductions detailing Lefty's career, Lefty took the podium and gave his standard opening.

"Call me Lefty," he said. He looked out over the crowd. They were smiling, waiting for his talk about baseball and the benefits of hard work and perseverance. "When I was just a kid growing up in Cutler, I learned to throw with either hand. But who ever heard of a pitcher named Righty?"

The smart aleck might have been drunk, but he delivered his line, loud and clear.

"What about *Righty Ford*?" the guy said.

The guy turned around in his chair with a grin, basking in the laughter of his friends.

Lefty had paused.

Gripped the podium with both hands.

Thought about it for a second or two.

"That's a good one, mister," he said. "*Righty Ford*. I'll be darned. Course, I weren't talking about *Yankee* pitchers, was I?"

The Elk Club members applauded Lefty.

Their wives applauded Lefty.

Even the liquored up smart aleck cheered.

❊ ❊ ❊

"I got three pitches," Lefty would say. "I

got my change-up, my slow change-up, and my knuckleball. Course I use the knuckleball about ninety percent of the time, and the rest of the time, I'm just waiting around in the bullpen."

When facing a true lefty, Lefty would switch his specially constructed glove to the right and pitch with his left hand. The umpires required him to let them know which hand he was using prior to the at bat, and wouldn't let him change hands on the same batter.

* * *

The sportswriters had written some nice things about Lefty in the Bangor paper when he retired, but it almost made Lefty feel as if he had died: *Lefty Gallagher played the game the Right Way*.

They wrote about the confusion faced by batters when facing Lefty's knuckleball: *Lefty Always Kept Them Off Balance*.

There was even a column about his speaking career: *Lefty Left 'Em in Stitches*.

* * *

Lefty kept a scrapbook with clippings from his career.

Those articles about his retirement were the

last ones he'd ever cut out.

* * *

The speaking engagements dried up, too. There wasn't much demand for washed-up minor league pitchers even if they were ambidextrous and funny.

* * *

"Put your things in the shed, Arthur," Olive said. "We'll have a full house this weekend. Move that trailer first, though. It's an eyesore."

"It's not a trailer, Olive," Lefty said. "It's a recreational vehicle, and I can stay in it if the place fills up. I don't need to use the shack."

"Let's not quibble about semantics right off," Olive said. "It needs to get moved. And that shed is not a shack."

"Kinda early for guests, isn't it, Olive?"

"These people are different. These people were kind enough to make a special call due to some extra-seasonal migration of the puffins. And they've already paid."

"Well, now," Lefty said, "that does make all the difference in the world, doesn't it?"

"Yes it does, Arthur," Olive said. "And I don't mind telling you so."

She looked at him again and gave him a half-smile.

"If I'd known you were coming, Arthur, I would have baked you a cake."

* * *

The birdwatching couple descended on the house in a car with Massachusetts plates.

Lefty watched the couple get out of their car. He watched the pale, bald man pull out luggage and camera equipment.

In profile, the man didn't look much different from a puffin.

Standing in the yard next door, Walter P. Jennings looked up from hosing his lobster traps.

"Looking for work?" Walter said.

The bald man laughed and turned to his wife.

Lefty knew what the man was thinking. Here was some local color they could tell their friends about when they got back home.

"You hear that, Helen?" the man said. "I can get a job here."

"Honey," his wife said, "I'd really miss you."

The couple were dressed in nylon clothing with

subdued colors appropriate for their hobby. They wore Rockport walking shoes, carried birding books, and they had deployed collapsible hiking sticks for the few steps from the car to the front steps of the inn.

Oh, they were going to be swell, Lefty thought. Just swell.

He looked at their car. It was a Saab. Even the car looked like it had a high IQ.

Lefty waved at Walter P. Jennings, who was still hosing the lobster tracks. Walter waved his hose in return, creating a rainbow over the traps. Lefty went back into his recreational vehicle. He'd driven the Winnebago all the way from Ormond Beach, just north of Daytona.

Lefty found it in *RV TRADER* and had paid cash for it from a man from Detroit who had just bought a house near an inland golf course.

Lefty had talked baseball with the man before any discussion of price.

Both were in agreement that the designated hitter rule was terrible for baseball, but now was probably here to stay. Lefty gave the man an autographed 8 x 10 portrait of himself, and the man looked very happy.

"I'm going to have this framed," the man said. "I'm going to put it up in the living room."

"Check with your wife," Lefty said.

"Can't remember if you ever came up to the plate or not," the man said. "I sure remember you with the Tigers, though."

"I hit," Lefty said. "I was a hell of a batter. Maybe better from the left side. But coming in like I did in relief, I never got too many at bats."

Lefty kept the same ocean motif with which the man and his wife had decorated the Winnebago.

Lefty liked the netting, cork and the tropical wallpaper. It gave the place a home-like feeling. Lefty kept the bar set up next to the kitchenette and used the juicer and blender a lot on his trip from Florida to Maine.

He kept potatoes and onions next to the small stove and steaks in the fridge.

It beat running into Denny's every night.

* * *

Back at the wharf, Lefty moored his boat to the wooden dock. He felt as if he had been home for days instead of hours.

Ricky Dunbar's boat was in the harbor. He'd take the birders out tomorrow. Maybe Ricky was the smart one. Run the tourists out to the island, show them some birds, bring them back.

How hard could that be?

Lefty walked back to the inn, cutting across the lawn where patches of grass were now ankle high. He would need to bring out the mower in the next couple of days before it got out of control.

The mail was nothing special.

A few catalogs and bills he'd taken care of from

Florida.

One interesting letter which contained what was being called a 'stunning offer.'

A man named Mordecai Carver planned to reform the House of David barnstorming team.

Carver wondered if Lefty would be interested in a tryout, or at least be willing to make a cash contribution.

An enclosed brochure showed a small group of men standing in scarlet baseball uniforms, each man with a beard approaching his naval. They looked somewhat happy to Lefty, but each of them had the glazed look of a fanatic.

Lefty threw the letter and brochure in the trash.

❈ ❈ ❈

Lefty made himself a cup of Nescafe on the Winnebago's hotplate

Buying the recreational vehicle had been a good move. He was glad to be out of Olive's way when she had guests. She had a tendency to become officious. He stood outside the Winnebago drinking the coffee, smoking a cigarette, and looking down at the bay.

The walk to the wharf took Lefty less than five minutes.

He'd called Jerry Sanders a couple of days ago. Jerry had already put Lefty's boat in the water.

* * *

Lefty was glad to be home. He put all thoughts of the winter in Florida out of his mind and looked in front of his big outboard. He would fish tomorrow, maybe do a little upkeep on the island.

Little River Island, guarding the mouth of Cutler Bay, grew larger as Lefty made his way out toward it.

WALK-IN COOLER

He had to get out of this thing.

Max Hellman realized he was in no danger of freezing to death in the walk-in cooler, but he also knew it was a matter of time before the cops would come in.

They would find him in here, wouldn't they? And what the hell could Max say?

He pictured himself being interrogated. What could he say that would sound reasonable?

He'd come in early. Seeing Tad had been shot he'd looked for the killers and inadvertently locked himself in the cooler.

What would he say after the cops stopped laughing? He would clam up. That's what he would do.

He would demand a lawyer, and eventually he'd get one. But that never really worked out. Anybody knew that. Usually, the court appointed lawyer would come in and just make things worse. They don't exactly send you Perry Mason.

He knew who'd done it. He knew who'd knocked

him out and dragged him in here. It was Bobby. Little punk that he was, Bobby had sneaked up on Max.

Max was beginning to remember things. He was remembering getting Iris to dance.

That had been nice, watching her. She didn't act so snobby when he had a gun, did she?

Then boom, boom, out went the lights.

There was no clock in the cooler and Max didn't wear a watch. It was dark as hell. Max had no idea how much time had passed.

He'd beaten on the cooler door, then stopped. There wasn't any point in it. He'd made himself something like a sandwich in the dark, but it really just amounted to some handfuls of bologna.

GROOVIN'

A few paint cans and some drop cloths were in the hall and Al had to step over them to get out of the walk-up apartment he shared with Max. Somebody was doing a mural. Al stared at it for a moment then kept moving down the dark hall. Even in the middle of summer, the hall was dark. The place smelled like boiling fish today. Al patted the pockets on his jeans and dug out a crumpled package of Newports. Lighted the flattened cigarette with a paper match. He carefully avoided touching the banister which always felt like it was covered in slime.

There were stacks of advertisers on the stairs where they'd been dumped this morning. The door to the outside came out next to the hardware store and Al looked carefully through the crack in the door before he came out. Al was not welcome in the hardware store any more. The big red-faced guy had made that clear, holding a pair of bolt cutters up to Al's nose. Al had been looking around and the guy figured he was shoplifting.

"Catch you in here again," the guy said, "the nose'll be the first thing I take off your worthless carcass."

Al had taken the guy seriously.

Max had laughed.

"He's joking with you, Al. That's how he is. You weren't kyping something, were you?"

Al had lowered his head.

"I guess maybe I was."

That made Max mad.

"Well, then whattya think's gonna happen, bro?" Max had pushed him. "What were you taking?"

Al shook his head. Shamefaced.

"Payday bar. That was it."

Max had laughed.

"I got your Payday, right here."

Making a joke of it.

Max had gotten over it, but the memory still hurt Al.

And Al still avoided the hardware store.

❊   ❊   ❊

Man, he was hungry. Al felt like he hadn't eaten in five days or something. He was thinking about Tad and how Tad sometimes filled up a skillet with scrambled eggs then added in the leftover meat from the doner kebab. Maybe Tad would do that today.

He smoked the cigarette, walking down the street. Hungry.

It was a beautiful day though. The sun was shining like crazy. Good day to go down to the park and lie out in the sun with your shirt off, catching the rays.

Maybe he'd do that after he caught up with Max and got something to eat.

He remembered that song by the Young Rascals. *Groovin'*.

Al couldn't imagine anything that was better.

Except maybe getting something to eat.

BOLOGNA AND SCHLITZ

Max had time to think, sitting there.

The look on Tad's face had been classic when Max walked in with the gun.

* * *

The chrome gun he'd gotten at the pawn shop on the outskirts of Mexico, Maine same time he got the big hefty one.

Raven 25 the smaller one said on the side. Chrome with some pearl grips. Simple to use.

He'd gotten the gun cheap. No chance you steal a gun.

Only Al would be dumb enough to try something like that.

After he'd bought the big gun, he'd seen the little one and asked the guy behind the counter if he could see it.

"I could put this in my boot," Max said. He'd seen that.

The guy sneered at Max. Smart ass, with a crossbow hanging in back of him a bunch of table saws and other crap in his shop.

"You could spend some time without your foot, too," the guy said.

He'd counted out Max's twenties. Looking at each one like there was something wrong with it.

* * *

Tad, looking up at Max, had tried to move the brown leather getaway bag which was lying out there on the table.

Tad hadn't been able to move it fast enough, so he just left it there.

Max had been aware for a while Tad was laundering money, he just didn't know it was this much. Max had tried talking to Boy Scout Bobby, figuring he'd at least know something about what big brother Tad was up to. Bobby just gave him the cold shoulder and pretended he had no idea what Max was talking about.

When he overheard Tad's conversation with the people he worked with, Max figured out when this money was coming in.

* * *

Tad had never given Max any kind of respect. He associated Max with Al, just because they shared a place and were both from Rumford. Tad figured any friend of Al's would also be some kind of waste case just like Al.

Al had been excited, getting the delivery job with Tad, like it had been some kind of opportunity.

His second day on the job he had come back to the apartment over the hardware store telling Max he'd talked to Tad.

Tad was going to let Max work there, too.

Thanks, Al.

Thanks for nothing, right? Until Max figured out how he could really make this job pay.

Meanwhile, there was at least a case of Schlitz the Bull in the cooler.

＊ ＊ ＊

Max felt somebody shaking his shoulder.

He looked up at Al's big goofy face. Al had turned the lights on in the cooler and Max's eyes took a second to adjust to the bright fluorescent light.

"Max," Al said. "Man, you won't believe it. Somebody shot Tad."

Max felt terrible. He'd already vomited and he smelled the pool of bologna and Schlitz on the floor of the cooler before he saw it.

"Help me up, Al," Max said. "I'm kinda stuck in here."

There was vomit all down the front of Max's shirt.

Al helped Max get up and out of the cooler. Max staggered toward the juke box.

Al pointed toward Tad's body which lay face up on the vinyl bench of the booth.

"Somebody shot Tad, Max," Al said. "Shit, look at him. It's unbelievable. Cop lady said to just sit tight. She said they'd get somebody here as quick as they could. I told her no hurry. I mean, he's dead, right?"

❊ ❊ ❊

Max went to the cash register and grabbed the key to the Gremlin underneath the counter where Max knew Tad kept his snake charmer.

He grabbed the short shotgun and a couple of shells next to it. Split the gun open and saw the .410 was loaded

"Let's go, Al," he said. "Gotta split, man."

He held up the key to the Taverna Athena delivery vehicle.

Al shook his head.

"I'm pretty sure we should stay, Max. That's what the lady said. She said they'd get here pretty quick.

Max heard sirens. Calculated how far the

Gremlin was from the front of the diner.

"Come on, Al. We gotta go. I'll explain later."

Al stood next to the jukebox. Slowly, he understood.

"Oh man, you didn't kill Tad, did you, Max?"

Max didn't have time to discuss anything with Al.

The .410 brought Al down.

Max wiped his own prints from the gun down before putting it in Tad's outstretched right hand.

DREAMING OF CLEVELAND

The luminescent hands of the Westclox read close to one o'clock in the morning when Lefty heard a voice and an insistent beating on the door of the Winnebago.

The beating intruded into Lefty's dream and awakened him.

Emerging from his dream, Lefty realized it was his sister.

Olive didn't sound frantic, but she kept repeating his name.

"Lefty, get up. You need to wake up. I'm not kidding."

Lefty rubbed his eyes. Checked the time again.

The dream was no great shakes. He had been circling a car inside a Cleveland supermarket parking lot. Lefty remembered the supermarket from his first stint with the the Indians. In the dream, Lefty had been unable to find a parking space, and then he couldn't find the home team's locker room.

"Wake up, Lefty," Olive said. "I need your help.

I'm serious."

Whatever the problem was, Lefty knew it had to be important.

Olive almost never called him Lefty.

KEEP YOURSELF ALIVE

The AMC Gremlin wasn't great for evasive action.

In some ways, it wasn't bad. Max remembered Tad bragging about his delivery vehicle, saying it could go from zero to sixty in twelve second. That was quick compared to some of the other cars on the road, but the Taverna Athena logo, a stylized Acropolis in Day-Glo green and black painted on the side, didn't exactly make the car inconspicuous.

Max knew he had to put the Gremlin some place out of the way where the give-away logo couldn't be seen on the sides of the already conspicuous car.

His head was starting to throb again. Max pushed the snake charmer under the seat, and stuffed the extra shells into the glove compartment. He knew if he were smart, he'd go throw the gun off a pier somewhere, but he didn't. When he found Bobby, he was going to need something to bring the little puke down.

He held Bobby responsible for Al's death. None

of that would have happened if Bobby hadn't sneaked up behind him like a little bitch.

Max turned through the narrow streets of South Portland. He had to find something close enough to the hardware store he could walk.

He felt nervous about getting a cab while carrying the snake charmer.

Out of the corner of his eye he saw the perfect place. He slammed on the brakes and threw the Gremlin into reverse, backing the car into the little alley opening just two blocks from his crib.

THE RAVEN 25

Olive pointed to the inn.

Lefty saw a woman standing next to the front door. Although the light in the entryway was dark, Lefty saw the woman was young, dark haired, and slender. He couldn't see anything more of her from this distance and in this light.

Maybe the woman standing next to the inn was in her late twenties? Late thirties? It was hard to tell.

Standing in the shadow created by the lilac tree next to the door, the woman reminded Lefty of someone he knew. At first he thought she'd been in the Cleveland dream. Lefty's recollection was dim. He couldn't remember who the woman was, or where he had known her. Lefty was barely awake, and this episode was also very much like a dream.

* * *

The woman had a suitcase next to her and she was steps away from the inn. In the driveway stood a Cadillac with its engine running. Lefty saw a young man in the driver's seat. The woman kept her face toward the inn, not turning back to the car. The guy got out of the car holding an overnight bag. Lefty couldn't see what the guy was doing, but when he went back to the driver's seat he was holding something that looked like a pizza delivery case.

"Go explain something to him," Olive said. She pointed to the Cadillac. "Maybe you speak his language. I know I sure can't get through to him. His name is Bobby. That was the only coherent thing I could get out of him. We don't have a room for him, that's for sure. You know as well as I do I can't take people in the middle of the night."

Olive stopped. Then lowered her voice and gestured toward the woman who stood on the porch.

"And her," Olive said. "She hasn't said a thing. Just got out of the car and walked toward the door with her purse."

Lefty ran his fingers through his hair and squinted through the closed screen door of the Winnebago.

"All right, Olive," he said. He held up his hand.

He was barely awake, standing in his boxer shorts.

"Give me a second to get some clothes on."

It was a starry night with a nearly full moon. There were a few lights from the boats in the harbor and Lefty could even see the island which stood sentry at the mouth of the bay.

Walking up to the Cadillac, Lefty got a closer look at the driver.

The kid behind the wheel gave Lefty a look.

Olive had said his name was Bobby.

He looked younger than the woman.

The kid's dark long hair, combed with oil, gleamed in the light from the moon. The expression on his face was challenging, as if daring Lefty to start trouble with him.

Bobby had on a jean jacket over a black T shirt. He looked like he was trying to prove something.

There was a gun on the seat next to Bobby. A cheap chrome plated job with the pearl handle grips. Lefty recognized it. A Raven 25 which would hold six cartridges in the magazine. Very common in Florida.

The gun could belong to the kid. It was cheap and flashy. You could buy one almost anywhere for fifty, sixty dollars.

The car probably didn't belong to the kid. It wasn't a young man's car.

Somewhere in the road behind him there had to be trouble.

What did Olive say his name was? Bobby.

Trouble brought him here in the middle of the night.

Traveling with a good looking woman. She was too old to be his girlfriend, too young to be his mother.

The Saturday night special would get him into trouble, if he wasn't in trouble already.

* * *

There were times Lefty felt Olive was losing a little bit of a grip on reality. And there were times when she just didn't pay attention.

Most of the time, Olive's reluctance to listen to Lefty seemed intentional.

This time though, she understood Lefty was telling her something very important.

Lefty stood directly in front of his sister, nodding his head almost imperceptibly toward the entry and pointing his finger. Certainly Olive would get the message. Lefty hoped he didn't have to spell everything out.

"Olive," he said. "Let's go ahead now and find this lady a room. Maybe the Spinnaker Room, is that open?"

Lefty faced his sister and raised his eyebrow as high as he could.

He inclined his head toward the Cadillac. Held the fingers of his right hand like a gun. He didn't want to play charades with Olive. Not in the middle of the night.

"Bobby needs to run a couple of errands. He won't be staying tonight."

Lefty forced himself to keep from clearing his throat.

He looked at the young woman more closely.

She was maybe in her middle to late twenties. Dark, attractive, tall and thin like a dancer would be. She was definitely older than Bobby, who was still sitting in the car. She was shivering, even though the night was still warm.

Then he recognized her, and wondered how he hadn't recognized Iris before.

Iris didn't say a word when Lefty spoke to Olive.

She looked as if she wasn't paying attention to their conversation, but that seemed unlikely to Lefty.

Iris was playing a part here. She was in trouble.

The gun on the car seat bothered Lefty. Hadn't Olive seen it? Or was that why she'd awakened him?

Olive understood what Lefty was telling her. Her grim expression changed slightly.

She looked at the Cadillac. Bobby sat motionless behind the wheel, the red ember of his cigarette on the bottom of the open window of the driver's side.

She turned back again.

"I see," Olive said to Iris. "I see. Well for heavens sake, let's get you in here."

Olive smiled at Iris. Taking her by the arm, she pulled her inside.

"We have a nice little room where I'm sure you will be very happy. It's not *The Spinnaker*. That one's not open yet. We call this room *The Princess Grace*."

❋ ❋ ❋

Bobby pointed at Olive.

"That woman," he said. "That's your wife?"

"My sister," Lefty said. "It's her place. She runs it. I'm just helping her out."

Olive was talking to the woman at the door.

"She's not letting us stay here," Bobby said. He pointed at the door. "What's that sign mean then? It says there's vacancies, right?"

Lefty nodded, looking at the kid's expression.

Guys like this were the same no matter where you went.

In Daytona Beach, St. Augustine, and before that in all the towns where Lefty had played ball, if the town was big enough, you would find guys like this one. Young guys with a Billy the Kid complex, looking to make their reputations.

Sometimes they carried guns like this one.

Maybe most of the time they carried guns, because they weren't hard to obtain, and guns made up for other characteristics they lacked.

Sometimes the ones in the pool halls and in card games were older than this guy. Every so often they were younger.

Lefty knew you had to be careful with this type if you wanted to stay healthy, just like you gave a wide berth to a rattlesnake.

Not because they were tough, but because they were not.

The kid's look wouldn't have distinguished him in a lineup. The long hair, the T-shirt and jeans.

Bobby drummed his index and middle fingers

on the steering wheel.

The diamond horseshoe ring was not on his pinky. It was on his ring finger, but fit loosely.

The kid probably had stolen the car. Maybe the ring, too.

Lefty looked at the Cadillac, looked back at Olive and then looked at the woman again. Was the woman part of Bobby's effort to look older?

Then Lefty brought his own empty hands deliberately up to the level of the Cadillac's window. He wanted to be sure Bobby could see them.

"It's a misunderstanding," Lefty said. "My sister makes mistakes. sometimes she doesn't even know what she's doing."

"I need a couple of things," Bobby said. He kept drumming his fingers on the steering wheel. "She says you're smart and can keep your mouth shut. Can you help me?

Lefty nodded.

"Can you?" The kid said.

"Probably," he said. "Might depend what those things you're talking about are. I'll help you if I can."

"Okay," Bobby said. He sighed deeply and pointed at the front door of the inn.

"It's worth some money to you if you can. First, the girl I'm with needs a room. Tonight and tomorrow night."

"That part's easy," Lefty said. "My sister already took care of that."

Lefty turned back toward the house. Bobby grabbed Lefty's arm.

"Wait," he said. "You got trouble hearing? I said I needed a couple things. The room's just one."

"Okay," Lefty said.

"I need a phone with nobody listening. That's one thing."

Lefty nodded.

"And I need a boat. Doesn't have to be a big one. I don't want one of those bastards down there."

Bobby pointed toward the harbor.

In just a couple of hours, the lobstermen would be heading out to check their traps. Ricky Dunbar, wearing his yellow slicker, coveralls and black glasses, would probably be coming up to the Inn to take Olive's bird-watching guests out to the far island way past the lighthouse to see the puffins and eiders, and gulls.

"I'm guessing you need the boat now," Lefty said.

Bobby nodded.

"You're a very smart guy," he said. "I guess it comes from living up here, right? All this fresh air? Is that what it is?"

"My sister's going to need a hundred and twenty for the two nights," Lefty said.

"Bullshit. I'll give her sixty, and that's plenty."

Lefty took the three twenties Bobby unfolded.

The bills were crisp and felt new.

FRIED CLAMS AND BLUEBERRY PIE

"Best let me into your car," Lefty said.

Lefty deliberately used a thick version of the Down-East accent Bobby might have heard on television.

He figured Bobby would expect the accent from him and Lefty didn't want to put the kid on guard.

Tourists loved hearing the accent when they came this far up the coast. Laughing about the way locals said things, maybe buying a *Bert and I* cassette tape to listen to in the car was as much a part of the Down East vacation as eating fried clams and blueberry pie.

Bobby gave an artificial grin in spite of himself. Patted the passenger's side of the seat of the Cadillac.

"Go ahead," he said. "Get in the *caaah*."

"Can you just hold on a second?" Lefty said. He gave an embarrassed look and held up his hand

and pointed to the Winnebago.

"Why? I haven't got all that much time."

"I gotta take a leak," Lefty said. He gave what he hoped was a loopy grin.

"Sure. But hurry up, wouldja?"

Lefty backed away from the car.

"Sure thing," he said, "I'll try."

Lefty didn't turn around. He didn't care if Bobby watched him or not.

Lefty only had a few minutes to do what he needed to do, and he needed to use that time properly.

❊ ❊ ❊

Inside the Winnebago, Lefty flipped on the overhead lights and retied his Converse Jack Purcells in the other-worldly cast of the fluorescent light. The canvas uppers and laces of the shoes were soaked by an early dew on the lawn.

He looked out from the windshield of the Winnebago. The lights from the second story hall inside the Inn were on.

Lefty saw Olive walking Iris down the hallway.

Carefully, Lefty supposed. Cautioning Iris to step lightly lest the birdwatchers be awakened. Welcoming Iris although nothing in this situation was normal.

Behind the wheel of the Cadillac, Bobby was smoking another cigarette.

Lefty grabbed his flashlight and switched off

the bright overheads. This was theater. He was putting on a show, and he didn't want Bobby to see the next part.

Lefty pressed the four digit combination on his gun safe. Took out his Smith and Wesson 29 with the blued four inch barrel. Carefully loaded the cylinder of the gun before putting extra cartridges in his shoulder holster.

His dark green Baxter State Park sweatshirt was a loose enough fit to cover the holster. Lefty pulled the sweatshirt over his head. The holster and gun wouldn't be noticeable under the bulky sweatshirt in the dark.

Above the guns in the safe, Lefty opened a cash drawer and pulled out a few twenty dollar bills. He fitted them into his worn billfold, slapped it shut and pushed the wallet into his hip pocket.

There was an opened roll of quarters on the console next to his steering wheel. Lefty kept the roll there for toll roads on the way to and from Florida. He grabbed the roll.

His field glasses fit in the left side pocket of his khakis. Not enormous binoculars like the bird-watchers used, these were compact, but powerful.

With his dark blue WaCo Diner hat askew on his head, Lefty rubbed his hands together coming out of the Winnebago.

Bobby looked at his watch.

"Took you long enough, don't you suppose?"

"Oh, sorry about that, mister," Lefty said.

The kid shook his head and gave a what-did-I-expect look at Lefty.

"Where's the phone?" he said.

"Well," Lefty said. "I been giving that some thought. I thought perhaps you could use Olive's, but then, you'd be pretty sure she'd be on the other phone, listening in. I know you don't want that. She can't help it, though, it's her nature."

Bobby nodded.

"Sometimes," Lefty said, "I might want to call a lady friend, but then Olive would be there on the other line."

"Where's the phone?" Bobby said.

Lefty pointed up the street, away from the wharf, down toward the mouth of the bay.

"Down there," he said. "If we drive, it's only two minutes. Might take longer to start your car than the time it would take to walk there, but I don't suppose you want to do that."

"No," Bobby said. "You're right. I don't suppose I want to do that at all."

* * *

Stretched across the front of the Marty's Cutler Store was a vinyl banner reading *MARTY'S FAMOUS SCALLOP SANDWICHES*.

Lefty pointed beyond the gas pumps. It was hard to see with the way the shadow fell across the building, but there was a pay phone in back of the gas pump.

Marty Flamond wouldn't let the regulars who gathered for coffee every morning use the phone he kept in the store. Even had there been an emergency, Marty would have pointed them out to the pay phone.

Marty's scallop sandwiches weren't as famous as the sign proclaimed them to be. Lefty didn't think the scallop sandwiches were particularly good, either. He preferred a fried egg sandwich to the scallops, and it wasn't because he didn't like scallops. Lefty just didn't care for the way Marty's wife prepared them.

Marty's wife put too much breading on the scallops, but you wouldn't want to tell her that.

"Just a second," Lefty said. He pulled the open roll of quarters out of his pocket and handed them to the kid.

"If you're calling long distance, you're going to need these. That's my guess, anyways."

Lefty shook the top of the roll of quarters. It was about half full.

"Take what you need," Lefty said, "You can be my guest."

Bobby hesitated, then accepted the roll from Lefty.

"Thanks," he said. "Stay right where you are, I mean it. We'll get the boat next.

Bobby got out of the car and holding the roll of coins, walked slowly past the gas pumps to the phone.

He really wasn't very old. Lefty guessed

seventeen or eighteen years old. A couple of years before this, Bobby could have been one of the local kids going into the store to buy baseball cards from Marty.

* * *

Lefty watched the phone booth while he pulled his bandanna from his pocket. Popping open the door of the glove compartment he quickly covered the bulb in the box partially with the bandanna. The registration and insurance were at the top of the plastic case.

Thaddeus Karras. A South Portland address. Not a street Lefty knew.

Probably the name of the kid's father.

There were a couple of service receipts in the box. Lefty took one of the receipts for a wheel alignment and quickly stuffed it in his pocket before closing the glove compartment. Bobby was still on the phone and was now feeding coins into the slot.

Lefty sat back in his seat and stood up straight.

At the phone booth, Bobby was talking.

LOBSTER POUND

Bobby got back into the car, slamming the door shut.

Something had happened during the phone call. Lefty didn't like Bobby's look. It was an ugly look made with lizard eyes, the kind you sometimes see in cheap dives after closing.

He was holding the thing he'd brought from the car trunk. It was a backpack. Every kid had one of these. Seeing Bobby with one of them made Lefty feel better.

"Hope you got nothing but good news, Bobby," Lefty said.

Bobby fished his keys out of his front pocket and turned the ignition. He looked over and blinked his eyes as if seeing Lefty for the first time.

"I'm not interested in conversation, buddy. Where's the boat?"

"Oh, that's easy," Lefty said. "Just turn this rig around and head up the other way. We're gonna head downtown, now."

Downtown.

The stretch along the bay was maybe a mile and a half back and there were five or six houses on both sides of the road. All of them were dark. Even the lights in the Summer Place Inn were now off.

Where the hell did Bobby want to go in the boat?

Bobby shook out a cigarette and passed the pack to Lefty.

Lefty pulled out his Zippo and a cigarette.

"I got my own," he said.

Bobby exhaled. He held his cigarette between his index finger and his thumb.

"You're name's Bobby?" Lefty said.

"Who told you my name?" Bobby said.

"Figured we should get acquainted, you're taking a late night trip and all."

The kid was worried. He was fidgeting behind the wheel. Erratic movement.

Whatever had happened, whatever brought him here, had affected him.

Bobby was trying to look and act tough.

Lefty could see Bobby was not tough, not really.

But Bobby was upset and trying not to show how upset he was, and Lefty knew that could be a dangerous combination.

Bobby turned to Lefty.

"You ever been out of this town?" he said.

"Once or twice," Lefty said. "I been down to Ellsworth. Bangor a time or two. Didn't think too much of either one."

Bobby nodded.

"Yeah, I don't know why I bothered asking you that. She said you were local. I just need a boat."

"In here," Lefty said.

He pointed to the entry to the wharf and a dirt parking space next to the lobster pound.

"Pull over there, you can park your rig and we can see about the boat."

Bobby pulled the Cadillac in and nosed it up to the dark concrete pilings along the wharf.

"What do you need the boat for," Lefty said.

"You don't need to know." Bobby said.

Lefty got out first. He stood looking at the bay.

Bobby sat behind the wheel of the Cadillac. He turned the lights off, got out of the car and stood next to the water.

❊ ❊ ❊

"You know how to run this?"

Lefty stood next to his boat. An eighteen foot aluminum runabout. It was stable in these water with a deep V bow. Nice red and white seats behind the windshield and wheel. And the Mercury provided more than enough power to get anywhere Lefty wanted to go along the coast.

Lefty wouldn't use anything but a Mercury.

"Of course I do," Bobby said. "I kinda grew up on the water."

"Going out in the middle of the night is different, ain't it?" Lefty said. "But I don't suppose you want to wait."

Lefty's veins felt like ice water. He was sure the

gun was somewhere on Bobby.

"You never saw me, buddy," Bobby said. "You don't know anything about this. Turn around and walk back up the hill to your place, and anybody asks, just say I went fishing."

He handed two twenties to Lefty.

"That's a lot of money, buddy, isn't it?" Bobby said. "Don't spend it all in one place."

"That ain't the plan at all, Bobby," Lefty said. "I'll take you out if you need to go out.

Bobby looked up at Lefty. Surprised.

"What, are you joking with me? I'll be back." Bobby patted the hull. "I'm not stealing this tub," he said. "I just need to get out to the island."

"Ain't saying you are," Lefty said. "Just need your keys to make sure of it. I'll take the money at the end."

"I just need to get out there," Bobby said.

He pointed vaguely at the dark bay.

"I'll bring this thing back in one piece."

"Get in then," Lefty said. "You ain't taking my boat."

Lefty held up the money. The two twenties Bobby had given him.

"I'll take the same amount of money when we get back. You come here in the middle of the night, you wake me up and you want to hire my boat. What the hell am I supposed to think?"

Bobby shook his head. Made an exasperated noise with his throat. Dug the keys out of his pocket and flipped them to Lefty.

"You don't have to think about anything," Bobby said. "I just need a ride out there."

Lefty looked at the black water around the boat. Bobby sat in the bow.

"I coulda saved you some money, Bobby," Lefty said. "I got a rowboat and a pair of oars. It's not far."

Lefty pronounced the words *not faah*, just for the hell of it.

Lefty guided the boat toward the island, weaving his way around the anchored lobster boats.

They were on the town side of the island. They wouldn't be able to see the lighthouse or the abandoned house of the keeper until they rounded the island.

Bobby sat facing forward next to Lefty.

"You should forget my name," Bobby said.

"What about Iris? I guess I should forget her, too?"

Lefty saw Bobby shrug.

"She's nothing. Don't stick your nose in where it don't belong."

"Doesn't take too long to get out there to the island," Lefty said. "Always surprises me. I don't know how many times I've come out, it always surprises me."

"Drop me off this side," Bobby said. "Don't go around all the way."

They were still on the side of the island with the trees. You couldn't see the lighthouse or the town.

"You wanna go through them trees?"

The lighthouse wasn't visible from the shore side. Even in daytime this was a bad landing spot.

"I can get you a little closer, Bobby," Lefty said, "but your shoes are gonna get wet."

THE DARK WATER OF THE OPEN BAY

Bobby knew how to get out of the boat. Lefty would give him that much.

He looked at Lefty and took two bills out of the backpack. Held out the forty dollars like he was offering ransom for a king.

"I gotta stay here," Bobby said. "It could take a while. You don't have to stick around."

Lefty nodded. The light was making an eerie pattern on the Bobby's face.

"You don't have to stay here," Bobby said.

"How you planning to get back? You planning on swimming?"

Bobby shook his head.

"You don't need to worry about that. You don't need to wait."

Lefty looked at Bobby who was clutching his backpack. Bobby was younger than Lefty had thought.

He stood in the moonlight, a skinny kid who might not even be old enough to legally drive.

"Listen, Bobby," Lefty said.

"Don't try giving me a lecture," Bobby said. He put his hand in the coat.

Lefty nodded.

"Sure," he said, "whatever you say."

"Listen," Bobby said. He looked at Lefty. "I'm sorry, man. Tell your sister too. I'm sorry."

Lefty shrugged.

"One more thing," Bobby said. "Listen, this is important."

He pointed back in the direction of the town.

"You got the keys to the Cadillac," he said. "I guess that's a good thing. Listen, I might be here a couple hours or a day. I don't know. You got the keys though. If I'm not back by dark tomorrow, you need to get into the trunk of the Cadillac. There's a bag in the back, brown leather. It belongs to Iris. Don't look in it, just give it to her. She knows what's in it, so don't try anything. Just give her the keys to the car. Tell her to take it."

Lefty waited and watched Bobby climb up the bank and cut through pointed fir trees growing behind the lighthouse.

There were stories about this place.

Lighthouse keepers raised their families on this island.

On summer days the kids would have been on the lawn until late evening hours chasing fireflies when the sun dropped.

"Take the car back to your place," Bobby said. "I mean, you already have the keys."

"That was my plan," Lefty said.

Lefty looked out at the dark water of the open bay.

Bobby had disappeared in the trees.

THE RUNABOUT

Lefty knew the island. The sun wouldn't be up for a while, but Lefty didn't feel right about this.

Many times during his high school years Lefty had used the little wooden peapod he had back to row out to the island. He'd gone out to the island with Danae Jennings to picnic and to watch the sun go down. It had been wicked easy rowing out to the island on a nice day.

The Lund runabout was far heavier than the peapod. Lefty had bought it years ago and it was heavy in the water. Practically indestructible even on the rugged coast. It would have taken all Lefty's strength to row the runabout out here, but he could row it for short distances.

Years ago, the Fresnel lens had been taken from the lighthouse lamp and the Coast Guard took over maintenance of the signal light.

An automatic light atop a skeletal tower meant a keeper was no longer needed on Little River Island. The last keeper had moved to the mainland years ago. The front of the island and the house were still maintained, but nobody was on the island permanently.

* * *

Lefty waited. There was something very wrong about this.

Something wrong about what Bobby had said.

Lefty moved to the center of his boat. He took the oars from where they were and quietly fit them into the oarlocks. Aluminum boats weren't quiet to maneuver, but Lefty didn't plan to go far.

When he reached the front of the island, Lefty dropped the oars. He could see Bobby.

Lefty checked his watch.

Bobby was sitting in front of the lighthouse on one of the gray granite ledges in front of the structure, staring east. Away from Lefty.

Bobby had the backpack between his knees.

Lefty shook his head. Whatever Bobby was going to do was out of Lefty's power.

All Lefty needed to do now was keep Iris safe.

He started the motor and headed back to Cutler.

BORN TO THE SEA

Bobby waited.

He saw Lefty out in the boat in front of the lighthouse. Bobby knew Lefty was watching him and so he waited until he was sure Lefty was gone.

Cold water wasn't an issue. It was dark, but Bobby fixed his eyes on the lights of the harbor. He didn't have to swim that far. He imagined a ninety degree arc from these lights and headed toward that shore on the opposite side of the bay from the inn.

Bobby and Tad were both good ocean swimmers. Tad taught him how to swim and they would laugh about the people watching them from the shore.

Wasn't it cold in there, the people would ask?

"We're Greek," Tad said. "We were born to the sea."

Bobby kept swimming. His body acclimating to the temperature of the salt water.

He remembered swimming with Tad.

Then he remembered his father and his mother.

They were long gone.

He remembered leaving Symi with them on the ferry to Rhodes to come to this country.

After they died it was only the two of them, Tad and Bobby.

Now Tad was gone and Bobby was on his own.

He kept swimming in the black waters of the bay.

✻ ✻ ✻

Cold and shivering, Bobby found the phone outside Marty's Cutler Store.

He lifted the receiver and dialed 911.

He told the dispatcher about his brother and the man who killed him. Described the Taverna Athena and the walk-in cooler.

Bobby hung up before there were more questions.

✻ ✻ ✻

After talking to the dispatcher, Bobby looked in the backpack. He divided the money into even amounts and left the leather bag in the trunk of the car.

Bobby's share of the money was in his backpack.

CALL ME LEFTY

Olive served a breakfast of scones, toast, bagels with jams and marmalades and some scrambled eggs she was calling a seasonal quiche. Somewhere, Olive had rounded up fiddleheads and put them into the eggs. Lefty came in and took a look at the breakfast and grabbed the carafe of coffee. He had taken a shower and shaved in the Winnebago and put on a fresh pair of khakis and a flannel shirt.

It seemed early for fiddleheads.

The coffee was good. Olive insisted on serving it in mismatched china teacups and saucers.

The female birder had come down for early breakfast dressed for foul weather. She was picking at the sides of the scrambled eggs like a small bird at a feeder.

"There's no meat in this, quiche, is there?" she said.

"Of course not, dear," Olive said. "You told me your dietary preferences over the phone, didn't you?"

"Are you sure you didn't include bacon?" the woman said. "Sometimes there's bacon. You ask for vegetarian, and the bacon still sneaks in there."

"No dear," Olive said. "There's not a scrap of bacon. Cross my heart."

Lefty went into the living room, separating himself from the birder by an open set of pocket doors and a potted fern.

He enjoyed drinking coffee while reading the sports section.

He glanced down at the water. The lobster boats were mostly out now.

Cleveland would be playing Detroit in a double-header this afternoon at Tiger Stadium. Oakland's game would start at around eleven o'clock Eastern Standard Time. Those were the teams he was most interested in.

Lefty never paid attention to the standings this early in the season. Teams were just messing around right now, as if the games didn't count yet.

Lefty pulled a Winston from the front pocket of his khakis. Snapped open his Zippo and thumbed the flint wheel.

The birder said something.

Lefty couldn't hear her. He put his hand up to his ear.

"I thought this was a smoke-free environment," the woman said.

Lefty stood up and walked out on the front porch. He looked down the street. Ricky Dunbar should have picked the birders up by now. They could be missing something. He puffed on the cigarette. The yard was not smoke free. It was a beautiful day. He could see the island in the distance at the far end of the bay.

He noticed Iris sitting on the porch swing, drinking a cup of coffee, looking at the ocean.

"Thanks for your help," she said.

Iris looked at Lefty and smiled.

❋ ❋ ❋

It was the same smile she'd given him when she waited tables up in Eastport.

The smile was the first thing he noticed about her.

He'd always liked the Eastport. He'd spoken there once to one of the men's clubs, back when he gave speeches. Then he'd gone back because he liked the place and it wasn't a long drive from Cutler.

The Diner had the usual setup with tables in the front and bar in the back. Some umbrellas out on the back deck for the tourists. Iris was still working there.

Lefty walked down Eastport's main street with her the night he'd cleared the guys out of the bar who were giving her trouble.

She had been shaky from the experience.

She'd asked him what his name was.

"Call me Lefty," he said.

She had laughed.

* * *

Lefty looked at her.

Something had happened which brought her here and took Bobby Karras out to the island.

Lefty sat down next to Iris and put his arm around her.

"You left him out there?" Iris said. She turned in her chair and was looking at Lefty. She wore a white blouse over a black swimsuit.

She took a cigarette from her purse. Lefty lighted it with his Zippo.

He watched her.

Iris looked scared.

"I did," Lefty said. "It was like he knew exactly where he wanted to go. Like he was meeting somebody. He said if he's not back by dark today to give you the keys and tell you there's a bag in the back of the car for you."

Iris raised her eyebrows.

"Did he take anything with him?"

"He took something. He had a backpack."

She shook her head.

"Who comes up here, anyway?" Iris said.

She looked at him again.

"What the hell happens here? Who stays in a place like this?"

Lefty laughed.

"You got me on that one, I guess," he said. "I suppose those of us who grew up here end up staying here."

Next door, Walter P. Jennings had come out of his house and was dragging his garden hose to another part of the yard.

"I should go out there."

"No," Lefty said, "he said he'd be back. He left me the key to his car for you."

"He won't be back. And I can't go back."

She turned away from Lefty, but not quickly enough for him to miss the tears.

"I'm not a victim here. I didn't have to come up here. He didn't force me."

Lefty looked at her.

"What are you doing?" he said.

"Bobby said this would work."

She held her head between her hands, rubbing her temples.

Lefty watched. She would tell him the story if he let her.

I figured things out about half way up here." She shook her head. "He had to get the money back to them. He worked for them."

She stood up.

"I'm sorry," she said. "I can't burden you with this."

Lefty nodded. He stood up.

"Walk with me," he said. "I'll take you to the car."

Her dark features were clouded by tears.

"Why can't you go back to Portland?"

Iris turned and faced Lefty. She blew a plume of

smoke into the air.

Inside, the birdwatcher's husband was sitting down to breakfast. Olive was hovering around the couple, replenishing their coffee and offering suggestions about things to do in the local area. Olive was good with light conversation.

"Stick around," Lefty said. "Bobby paid for two nights. And I'm not giving you the keys until it's dark."

She looked out over the bay. The sun glinted on the water making visible now the lobster buoys .

"I'm sorry about what I said about this place. It's nice here, isn't it?"

Lefty pointed at the couple still inside at the table.

"You could go out with them. They're birdwatching. Puffins, egrets, all kinds of birds."

She looked down.

"Help me," she said. Lefty could barely hear the next words. "They're going to kill me."

Lefty stood up. He took Iris's wrist and pulled her from the chair.

"Let's go," he said.

"What are you talking about?" she said.

"I'm taking you out there."

❋ ❋ ❋

Walter P. Jennings was still washing down the lobster traps and barely looked up when Lefty and

Iris passed his house.

Iris had put on shoes and Lefty was taking her down the street to the now active wharf.

"Who are these guys?" he said.

She didn't answer.

They were on the steps leading to the the little beach. The Cadillac still stood next to the concrete pilings where Bobby had parked it the night before.

Lefty saw a piece of green sea glass. He picked it up. The glass had worn to an oval shape.

He handed it to Iris.

"You're sweet," Iris said.

She took Lefty's hand and he guided her down the steps.

✽ ✽ ✽

She held his hand again when he helped her into the boat.

"I've never been out in a boat like this before," she said.

"Stick around," he said.

The runabout looked better in the daylight, cutting over the water of the bay. Lefty enjoyed being with Iris. She had put on a white sweater and wore sunglasses and sat next to Lefty as he powered the boat to the island.

"He said not to come out until dark?" she said.

"It's a free country, last time I checked," Lefty said. "If he needs help, I can help him."

"You don't know that," she said.

* * *

Lefty circled the island in the boat. Did a scan of the beach.

Lefty helped Iris from the boat.

"The island with all the puffin's another couple miles out there. Those birdwatchers will be out there for a while."

There was a cigarette butt next to the bench where Bobby had sat. There was no other sign of Bobby.

"Stay here," Lefty said. "I'm looking around."

Iris sat on the bench. She had said nothing since arriving on the island.

"He could still be here," she said. "He could be out in those trees. Maybe he's hiding."

"Believe me," Lefty said. "If he's here, I'll find him."

Iris shook her head.

"I don't think he's here," she said. She was trying not to cry.

"There's something going on here, Iris," Lefty said. "You want to tell me about it?"

She looked at him and he waited.

"They're going to look for me," Iris said. "They're probably looking for me now. I know who they are."

"Give me some names," Lefty said.

"Why?" she said. "They were just some guys. Max and Al were their names. Is that what you want?"

Iris looked up at Lefty.

"Where was this," Lefty said.

"I worked for Bobby's brother down in Portland," she said. "The Taverna Athena. Bobby ran the place in the mornings for Tad. I waited on tables. These guys Max and Al worked for Tad. Delivery guys. I think they robbed Tad. I know Max killed him. Bobby got there later. He was trying to protect me, I think."

In the distance, Lefty saw Ricky Dunbar's boat going out. Out to see the puffins. A perfect day for birdwatching.

She looked down. She was going to cry of course. Once she got started, it would be hard to get much more from her.

"Bobby tried," Lefty said. "He probably *was* trying to protect you."

She shook her head.

"He was," she said. "That's why he's dead."

"You don't know that he's dead."

"Where could he have gone? He's dead."

Might as well let her cry, Lefty thought. She could be right.

If Bobby had tried to swim away from the island he probably would have drowned.

Maybe somebody had picked him up off the island. That was doubtful. It would have taken hours for anyone Bobby knew to get to the island,

and the currents here were unpredictable even for the local fishermen.

Lefty watched Iris cry.

It was inevitable. Maybe it was better that way.

Of course, it was better that way.

He watched the tears start. Then a gasp. Then anguish.

She wouldn't tell him anything more now. He would have to wait.

Lefty touched her shoulder and then he held her.

He felt the fear in her body turn to grief.

AN ENCAMPMENT OF GYPSIES

"That's a vulgar display, Arthur," Olive said.

A small shower had started. Early summer rain, the kind which occurs in full sunshine. The rain had given no notice, and wouldn't last.

Lefty and Olive sat together at the dining room table.

Iris had gone to the front of the inn and stood among the flowers.

Lefty had made himself a tuna sandwich and Olive had a bowl of bouillon with melba toast. The birdwatchers were still out with Ricky Dunbar on the two-day puffin tour.

Ricky had arrived delivering apologies and excuses. The birdwatching couple had been perturbed, but Ricky did his best to assure them this was the best time to see the puffins.

"What's vulgar, Olive?"

Olive pointed outside where Bobby's black

Cadillac was parked.

Iris's Cadillac now.

"The trailer is one thing, and the Cadillac is another. But put them together, it looks like an encampment of gypsies. And I happen to know what a gypsy camp looks like, so don't contradict me."

"First," Lefty said, "it's a recreational vehicle, not a trailer. Second, I happen to have known a lot of gypsies in my career. That's not their style."

"Fine," Olive said, "have it your way, if you must. But it's vulgar. It makes us look like we're running a carnival. And we are not."

Lefty nodded, then took another bite of the sandwich. He was barely listening to Olive. He watched Iris. The rain had stopped for now. A rainbow had appeared in the distance.

At some point, Iris might tell him more.

GUS PAPPAS

Gus Pappas didn't like picking up the phone this late at night. You never knew what you were going to hear about. He rolled to the edge of the bed and grabbed the receiver before it awakened his wife.

She was asleep still.

"Yeah," he said.

Mike on the other end. Sounding tired, but it had to be important.

"Tad's dead," Mike said.

"What're you talking about," Gus said. "He was fine this morning."

"He ain't fine now. His delivery guy shot him. You saw him. The dipshit came in when we were there. He took the money. Cops got there on a tip. I found *that* out from a friend of a friend. Two guys are dead, Tad and another guy. The other delivery guy. Money's gone. This guy Max had to take it."

Gus looked out the window at the dark summer night. Three trees on his front yard and a white iron fence.

"Tad's little brother know about this?"

"I don't think so," Mike said. "Not yet. Poor kid. Probably out on the beach picking up chicks or something and he's got no idea. He's that age."

"That's tough for him, though," Gus said. "Tad was like his father."

Mike cleared his throat.

"You want me to take care of this?"

"Yeah," Gus said. "You do that."

THE WESTCLOX

Lefty woke up quickly.

He knew it was Iris.

The Westclox said it wasn't yet midnight.

Lefty opened the screen door on the Winnebago.

"Let me in?" she said.

She stood in the yard with her profile in the moon.

Lefty stepped down and took her in his arms. He kissed her. She was starting to shake.

She pulled away.

"They're going to find me," she said.

Lefty looked at his watch.

It was midnight.

"They won't find you," Lefty said.

He stroked her black hair. He felt her shaking decrease, replaced by hungry insistence.

"They won't find you. You're safe with me."

He kissed her again..

She stepped away.

"I'm not safe," she said.

Lefty looked at Iris from arms length.

"You need to tell me what's going on," he said.

"Have you got a cigarette? I left mine inside."

Lefty shook two cigarettes from his pack.

"I need the keys to the Cadillac."

Lefty nodded.

"I'll get them for you."

"I've got to leave. These guys are rough. I don't want you to get hurt."

Lefty shook his head.

"I'm not going to get hurt, and neither are you," he said. "But you gotta trust me, Iris."

He led her to the folding chairs in front of his Winnebago.

They both sat down. Neither said a word.

They looked at the stars above the bay.

"What do you hear?" she said.

There was only the lapping sounds of the surf in the distance.

"Shh," Lefty said. He held his finger over his lips.

"Lefty?" she said.

He looked at her.

She pointed at the Winnebago.

"I'd feel safer in there."

❉ ❉ ❉

"I shoulda listened to my sister," Lefty said. "She told me to move the car."

Iris looked out the window of the Winnebago at the Cadillac.

"Tad just bought that car."

"I had a Cadillac once," Lefty said. "I traded it for a Bronco."

"He told you to give it to me?"

"If he didn't show up, you were supposed to get the car. That's what he said."

"Bobby always joked with me, saying he was going to buy me a car some day. I told him I wanted a Thunderbird convertible or nothing."

She stopped. Looked at Lefty.

"He was such a kid," she said.

"I guess you got a Cadillac instead."

Iris shook her head.

"Is that even legal?"

Lefty shrugged.

"Probably," he said.

She cried again. Lefty held her.

Then she stopped and dried her eyes.

Lefty wasn't going to hurry her.

"I worked at Bobby's brother's restaurant in South Portland."

"You told me a little about that," Lefty said.

"It was a nice place. Tad was Bobby's older brother. He acted like his dad."

She pointed at Lefty's pack of cigarettes.

"May I?" she said.

"Help yourself," Lefty said. "You don't have to ask."

She lighted the cigarette. Her hands trembled a little.

"They're both dead. I can't believe it. Bobby. He was just a kid. He and I goofed around. Bobby liked to play like he was a big man and he was going to take me away. I let him kiss me a couple of times. More than a couple of times. He was sweet, but he was a baby."

Lefty kept quiet, letting her talk.

"Tad was dead when I came in yesterday morning. He was lying in one of the booths. Max was sitting there with the gun in his hand."

"This guy Max. Who is he? You said something about another guy."

"Max and Al work for Tad. They make the deliveries."

"What happened after you came in?"

"Bobby came in, thank God. He whacked Max over the head with a pool cue. He dragged Max into the cooler. Then we left."

"Why do you think Max killed Bobby's brother?" Lefty said.

He picked up the pack of cigarettes and pulled out his Zippo.

She shook her head and exhaled. Put the cigarette down.

"There was money," she said. "Bobby grabbed a leather case when we left. He put Max's gun in the case, but there was money in there. I saw it. More money than Tad made at the diner. A lot more."

Lefty interrupted.

"Bobby knew about the money in the bag?"

"He must have, right? He knew a hell of a lot. Me, I didn't know anything. Not the whole time I was working there."

"Let me guess," Lefty said. "Tad laundered money? Is that right?"

Iris propped her chin up. "Maybe. I never saw it. It's probably a good guess. I don't know. I just worked there."

"Like Bobby and Max and the other guy."

"Al," she said.

"Al," Lefty said. "You all worked there."

"Bobby thought he could protect me" she said.

Lefty remembered the gun.

.25 caliber. A pearl handled Falcon.

Sixty bucks at a pawn shop near you.

"You ended up here," Lefty said.

She looked at him.

"I'm glad you did," he said.

THE ALLEY

Max figured the time was very tricky. Get out of the apartment, people could be looking for him. Stay inside, police arrive. Pick you poison, you could say.

He watched the *Space Invaders* cascade down the screen of the television. He was out of food. Al should have gotten some, but he hadn't.

It wasn't going to be the same without Al. They'd known each other forever. But in a way, Max figured, it was probably for the best.

He was hungry. He figured he could go get an Italian sandwich. The place he liked going to would be open.

He walked down the hall, stepping over the paint cans.

His head wasn't feeling half bad, now. He'd gotten some rest.

Max walked down the stairs and past the hardware store. Closed for the night but the lights were still on.

In the alley, he opened the door of the Gremlin and got behind the wheel.

He stopped. Realizing he'd forgotten

something.

He had left the Snake Charmer up in the apartment.

This realization came at the same time Mike Pappas rose from the back seat of the Gremlin and pointed the business end of his Cobra .38 into the back of Max's skull.

DIRTY MONEY

The Bold Coast stretches along Down East into the Bay of Fundy. The promontory rocks and pointed fir trees are shaped by rugged winters and unforgiving tides. If a body was left out here between the rocks in the right time of year, that body would never be found. Between unforgiving tides and scavenger birds no trace of the unfortunate corpse would remain by the following summer.

Lefty put the big rocks into the brown leather bag.

The same rocks where he and Iris watched the sun come up only a few days before. Bobby had likely died at sea.

He and his brother had died for no good reason.

❉ ❉ ❉

Iris looked at the money in disbelief when Lefty unzipped the bag.

Riches.

The bag had been in the back of the car, just

where Bobby had said. Lefty hadn't looked into the bag before showing it to Iris.

It was dirty money, but it didn't have to be that way, Lefty told her.

There was nothing bad about the paper and ink. It was just money.

Iris would be able to give this money a clean future.

Lefty pushed the leather bag down deep into a crevice between two rocks. The bag fit snugly, and Lefty covered it with balsam boughs. The balsam tips were fragrant.

Lefty looked around.

Winter would be here before long.

EARLY TO RISE

Gus was waiting with his clubs when Mike pulled up.

"Jeez Louise, Mike," Gus said. "Takes you long enough."

Mike grinned.

"We got time. We got an eleven o'clock tee time. So we get breakfast, some coffee, I don't know what. Besides, I was the one took care of things last night. I should be sleeping in."

"Early to rise is healthy, Mike."

Mike nodded.

"So is early to bed, and I didn't get back home till I don't know when. Kathy was wondering what I was doing."

"She shoulda called me. How long you spend with that clown?"

"Forty-five minutes I'm in the Gremlin just waiting for him to show up. You know what kinda back seat they got in those things? They're nothing. I was cramping up like you wouldn't believe. Then, I gotta drive him around while he's blubbering."

"No shit?" Gus said. "He have the money?"

"No, that's the thing. The whole time he keeps saying 'Bobby did it. Bobby did it,' like he's a record with the needle stuck."

"Uhn-uh," Gus said. "Bobby didn't shoot Tad. You know that as well as I do. Bobby's family. He's a good kid."

"Don't I know that?" Mike said. "Finally, I get Max to admit to the shooting. Turns out he not only shot Tad, but this creep also shot his partner. He sounded kinda proud about that, too. But all the time he's still talking about Bobby taking the money. 'Bobby did it. Bobby did it.' That's all he'll say. He stuck to that pretty good."

"That's it then? What about the money?"

"Be patient," Mike said. "That's when I figured it out."

Gus looked at his brother. Mike was wearing a yellow and white sweater today over yellow slacks.

He was grinning at Gus.

"What did you figure out, Mike? Let me in on it."

"Yeah, okay, I was getting to that. So, Bobby *did* take the money, and we should be happy he did."

Gus looked at him.

"I don't follow."

"Bobby's a bright kid. He's gonna take over Tad's business, right? He sees what happens, you think he's just gonna leave the money there for the cops or whoever shows up? Uhn-uh. Like you said. Bobby's family. He'll bring it back when the heat's off. Thing of it is, by taking the money when he did, Bobby saved us some trouble. Cops see that bag of dough, that's the last you and me see of it."

Gus nodded.

"Hope you're right, Mike. I just hope to hell you're right."

Gus pushed his brother's shoulder.

"Course I'm right, Gus," Mike said. "Bobby's family."

"What about Max?" Gus said.

Mike grinned again.

"You don't have to worry about Max," he said. "Ain't nobody gonna find old Max without scuba gear."

Gus grinned.

SAINT NICHOLAS

Bobby took the last few strokes and touched the rocky cliff with his hands. Pulling himself hand over hand until his entire body was out of the water. He stood up, clearing his eyes, nose and ears. He felt the sun shine on his body and smelled the wild sage filling the air. He started to climb the hill. It was a tough climb, surprisingly so.

The salt water felt good in Symi.

No more cold water swims like the last one in Cutler.

Bobby wondered what Tad would have said about his trip.

Bobby had taken his passport and half of the money, and returned home to the island.

Boston to Athens to Rhodes. Then a ferry to this island he barely remembered.

Would Tad have been proud of Bobby?

Bobby shook the last of the salt water out of his hair which now fell to his shoulders. He was at the island's highest point. From here he could see Saint Nicholas Beach.

On the other side of the mountain the ruins of windmills still stood upon a ridge of hills. Bobby had run on this hill as a child.

His grandparents were still living in the village. Old, but they were still living.

They had kissed Bobby and taken him to the other side of the island where Saint Michael's Monastery had stood for centuries.

They celebrated with an enormous meal and by singing songs Bobby only understood in his heart.

He gave most of the money to his grandparents, telling them the money came from Thaddeus.

CONVERTIBLE THUNDERBIRD

Lefty usually left Cutler before Thanksgiving.

He had enough memories of winter to carry him through Christmas. He could close his eyes and see Cutler. Dry-docked boats wrapped in white. Clapboard houses gleaming with red and green lights. Snow.

He left while the trees were still in full foliage. When the leaves fell the snow would arrive. Today, there was a chill in the air and it felt like fall.

He looked at the postcard which had come in the mail. A lobster with steamed corn on the cob and a dinner roll on a checked tablecloth. On the back, Lefty read the message written in green ink.

Dear Lefty,
Come see me at my new cafe. Some things don't change. Anyway, all's well that ends well.
Love
Iris
PS: Thanks a million for your help!

She wrote the name of a town under her name.

Lefty put the card on the dash board of the Winnebago. He took out his Zippo, lighted a cigarette, turned the key in the ignition and drove out of Cutler. The inn was shut for the winter. Olive would stay a while longer, but she would also head south eventually. Lefty would see her again next summer.

* * *

It was on Main Street in a picturesque town right off Highway 1.

Iris's Cafe.

Iris saw him from the back, smiled at him and brought him a menu.

"You found the place, Lefty," she said. "I'm glad."

Not far from the water, but not too close. The cafe was nice, but there would still be plenty of work for her to do on the place. She might need help. There would be time for all of that.

He looked down the street. There was no sign of a Cadillac. Instead, parked on the corner was a convertible Thunderbird.

McIndoe Falls, Vermont
July, 2020

Thank you for reading this book.

If you enjoyed *Lefty and the Killers,* please consider writing a short review on Amazon or Goodreads.

Also, please tell your friends.

As Walter Tevis, writer of *The Hustler* and *The Queen's Gambit* wrote when making the same request: "word of mouth is an author's best friend and much appreciated."

Trevor Holliday

Printed in Great Britain
by Amazon

25888311R00098